MAGGIE HEMINGWAY

Maggie Hemingway was born in Orford, Suffolk. After an early childhood spent in New Zealand she returned to England and now divides her time between London and the Kent coast. She worked for some years in publishing before becoming a full-time writer. THE BRIDGE, her first novel, was published to considerable acclaim and won the Royal Society of Literature's Winifred Holtby Prize. She has since had published two further novels, STOP HOUSE BLUES and THE POSTMEN'S HOUSE, and is now working on her fourth novel.

sceptre

Maggie Hemingway

THE BRIDGE

British Library C.I.P.

Hemingway, Maggie
  The bridge.
  I. Title
  823[F]

  ISBN 0-340-56533-0

Printed and bound in Great Britain for Hodder and Stoughton Paperbacks, a division of Hodder and Stoughton Ltd., Mill Road, Dunton Green, Sevenoaks, Kent TN13 2YA. (Editorial Office: 47 Bedford Square, London WC1B 3DP) by Clays Ltd, St Ives plc.

Author's Note

In 1884, having completed his studies in Paris, the painter Philip Wilson Steer made for Walberswick, a tiny village on the Suffolk coast. Until 1887 he spent every summer there alone, formulating his own style of English Impressionism. In 1888 he persuaded a painter friend, Fred Brown, to join him, and by 1889 their visit to Walberswick was sandwiched in between trips to Montreuil-sur-Mer and Boulogne. They visited Walberswick briefly for the last time in 1891. After that Steer's summers were always spent in the company of other painters, journeying all over Britain in search of suitable painting places. His style, too, seemed to change: he never again painted with the same vitality and freshness, or handled paint in such a sensual, direct manner as he did in the Walberswick years. Was it possible that he just became tired of this beautiful place? Or did something else make Walberswick unbearable for him? When Steer died at 82 of bronchitis, still a bachelor, surrounded by his cats and his Chelsea china in Cheyne Walk, London, his private papers were, according to his wishes, thoroughly disposed of, and there is nothing in the archives that remain to throw any light on the private life of this very private man. The events in this novel are, therefore, pure speculation. All other characters apart from Walter Sickert, Charles Shannon and Dolly Brown are fictitious. All place names mentioned, however, are real, though licence has been taken with the exact location of Foxburrow Wood.

Chapter One

Emma was determined to be first into every room of the new house, running in a kind of delirium up every staircase and along every passage that presented itself to her. The sight of white china doorknobs gleaming untried in shadowy lines whipped up further the hysteria of discovery and made her shriek every time she burst into another room, without even hearing that she did so, stumbling against pieces of furniture as she ran across the floor, pressing herself briefly against the window, then turning and racing out again to hurl herself at the next door.

In her progress she would frequently bump into servants slowly negotiating narrow corners carrying tin trunks, or stumbling up unfamiliar stairs with mountains of linen. And she would dart between and behind them, leaving them muttering sourly after her. She heard her sisters, too, far behind, peevishly calling her, their voices fading into rooms and emerging again on a lower staircase. But she was driven on ever higher, until at last she flung open a door at the very top of the house and rushed across to the window. Instantly she stretched wide her arms against the cold glass, as though to gather all that she saw into her, whispering with a profound longing over and over again, 'The sea, the sea.'

That was where her sisters found her some minutes later, gazing out to where a faint blue line lapped against the sky between hillocks and sand-dunes.

'Look!' exclaimed Emma, turning towards them with an expression of great pride and achievement.

'What?' They pushed her aside. 'Move over, Emma.'

Maria peered over her shoulder and pouted. 'Pity we can't see the beach for the sand-dunes.'

'I'm going to sleep here,' Emma announced, clutching desperately at the last inch of sill. She could hardly see the sea at all now, and pushed back at her sisters to regain her claim.

'Stop shoving, Emma!'

'This is *my* window!'

'This is not your window, we're looking out of it now.'

Sophie and Maria linked arms along the sill and giggled at each other.

'Except for the road and that bit of meadow in between, you might almost think the sea was just at the bottom of our garden,' Sophie said loudly to Maria.

'Part of our seaside estate, you mean. Like Victoria Moran's trout lake!'

They giggled again.

'This is my bed,' said Emma in a loud voice. She had given up tenure of the window and was sitting on a little truckle bed in a corner of the room, plucking uncertainly at the black and white ticking of the mattress. 'I'm going to sleep here.'

'You can't sleep here,' said Sophie over her shoulder.

'Yes, I can.'

'No, you can't.'

Maria turned from the window in exasperation. 'This is a maid's room. Mama would never allow you to sleep here.'

Suddenly deprived of all her trophies, Emma burst into tears.

'This room is for servants,' hissed Maria, goading her, 'and you can only sleep in it if you are a servant. Is that what you want to be? A little servant – ?'

She stopped. In the doorway stood a young girl in a starched cap and apron, holding a small battered brown cardboard suitcase. She put the case down and stared at Emma.

'What's wrong, Miss?'

'Go and tell Mama Miss Emma is having a rage,' Maria ordered, and turned back to Sophie.

Emma flung herself, sobbing, on to the bed.

The maid found Mrs Heatherington sitting on one arm of a sofa in the drawing room, holding a small blue travelling hat in her lap and staring out into the garden through the glass doors. She seemed quite oblivious of the commotion in the hall and on the stairs – of the shouts of the carter's men, and the squawking of the maids as the London maids directed the country maids as to the contents of each box and the country maids tried to direct the town maids to the appropriate room,

8

neither side understanding the other, so that there was nothing but confusion in the house.

'Ma'am,' whispered the maid, afraid to interrupt her mistress's composure.

But Isobel did not hear her. She sat in a kind of trance, her eyes focused on a blurred spot in the pink and red brickwork of the wall at the far end of the garden, not quite seeing the sun-shadowed leaves of the fruit trees fanned out along its length or the clematis twining among the heavy sprays of roses that nodded against it. For she could not bring herself to arrive. She twisted her hat in her hands as though she would in an instant put it on again, jump up and stride out. She saw London still, in images that overlaid the calm of the garden. Her house in the stuccoed square, with carriages at the door and the bustle and hastening of her husband to set them off on their journey, his own eagerness to leave for the City, the strange absence of farewells. She had no desire to be there. But where was here? It was a place that everyone else seemed to know about, save Isobel. Her aunt had recommended it, her husband had engaged it, the driver of the chaise and the carrier's cart which had followed them from the station had arrived at it without hesitation. And *it* knew all about her. Its maids and cook and scullery girl and gardeners had all been waiting in a line at the exact second that the chaise drew up on the gravel drive outside the house. There had occurred a moment of embarrassed silence – the little girls hushed by the presence of the ill-assorted reception committee, the committee over-awed by their London visitors – before Isobel realised that she was now expected to get out. Here was the destination they had planned for her. No one else seemed to have the slightest difficulty in accepting this, so why couldn't she? Her unwillingness to descend from the chaise was a tiny, momentary thing; but it was noticed, as such things are, by the servants. And when they talked of her in years to come, as they did from time to time, they would shake their heads, purse their lips and point to that second of unwillingness, saying that it had significance.

'Ma'am,' the servant tried again, and this time the woman's head turned slowly with a small, surprised smile, as though she had been woken out of a dream.

'What is it?' inquired Isobel.

'One of the young ladies said I was to tell you Miss Emma's having a rage.'

'A rage?'

'Yes, ma'am.'

'Oh dear,' sighed Isobel. She placed her hat lingeringly, reluctantly, on the chair beside her, unable quite to brush out her indecision with the creases in her skirt as she stood up.

'Where are they?'

'Upstairs, ma'am. On the top floor.'

As Isobel reached the first landing a maid emerged from one of the rooms.

'Excuse me, ma'am, but we can't tell where to unpack for the young ladies, nor which beds to make up.'

'I'll be down directly, Nancy.'

As Isobel turned to mount to the second floor she felt the cold smoothness of a carved dolphin's head under her fingers on the newel post. Sunlight shone in through a deep sash window halfway up the stairs, burnishing the dark panelling on the walls and the waxed and polished staircase. The balusters, she now saw, were notched and curled as though entwined with seaweed and shells. Set into the walls at intervals were pairs of joined fan-shaped brass shells, half-open in a delicate intimacy to reveal not the tiny sea-creatures that might inhabit them, but candles. She climbed higher into another splash of sunlight from another long window. It seemed very calm and warm up here, muffled noises from the floors below floating up the stairwell as though through water, the dolphins and the chiselled curls of seaweed following in her wake until she reached the last flight of stairs.

Here the polish and the ornament ceased abruptly. The stairs were now bare wood, dried white and splintered like the planks of a ship. From the narrow landing, passages led off to left and right like rough-hewn caves. In the patch of sunlight at the top of the stairs tiny motes of dust danced up and down, glittering, never falling out of the web of light in which they were imprisoned. Isobel stopped and put her hand into the sunlight, but the dust danced on over the back of her hand and between her fingers, undisturbed, as though she did not exist. And then, from one of the passageways, she heard Emma sobbing.

When she located the room she was taken aback for a second

by the scene before her – Emma weeping loudly on a stained mattress in one corner, and across the bare, uneven floorboards Sophie and Maria turning slowly from the window, their eyes meeting conspiratorially as they turned, their faces sulky with guilt. Then Maria, vociferous, drowned out Emma's sobs with a catalogue of Emma's sins, and Emma, leaping up with a sobbing shriek of rage at such unfairness, hurled herself at her mother as though to force justice out of her.

'Mama, they took my window. They pushed me out and wouldn't let me look . . .'

'It's not your window,' snapped Maria.

'Show me,' said Isobel, taking hold of one of Emma's clutching hands and putting the other arm round Maria, sweeping across the room towards the window with them. Maria's shoulder dragged against the movement, hunching and turning as though to break free. They stood unwillingly together and looked out through the dusty glass, Emma elated by repossession of her domain, Sophie and Maria feigning uninterest, and Isobel, who could not prevent the sudden sinking of her heart.

'Look! Look!' squealed Emma, jigging up and down, holding tight to the window ledge. And they looked at the empty landscape before them.

It was a landscape of cloud-swept sky and wind-blown grass. Across the road there stretched a flat meadow that sank quickly into marsh, whose watery beginnings were marked by reeds waving in sinuous ripples of brown and grey and green. Behind the marsh rose a line of sand-dunes, dipping and rising in a long curve right along the bay, two miles or more, to Dunwich. They could just see over the top of them to where the sea lay, blue and glittering far out, until it faded into a thin line and the sky began, pale with the eternity of summer. On the opposite side of the road, the only other house visible was built of the same crumbling rose-coloured brick, in the same perfect rectangle as their own, only slightly smaller and sinking below the level of the road as though it were already a victim of the marsh that lay behind it. To their right, the road disappeared towards the village; to their left, it ran level for three or four hundred yards to end in the estuary, where the ground shelved sharply so that the water overlapped the top of the Hard and, at high tide, crept up to the stilts of the black tarred fishermen's huts built around the quay.

'Can you see the sea, Mama?' breathed Emma. 'Isn't it lovely!'

It was the sea that gave Isobel at last a sense of destination, the sheer practicality of seeing the end of the land, battlemented with sand-dunes against the beginning of the sea, that made her realise she could, in fact, go no further.

'There's not a soul in sight,' murmured Sophie.

'What happens if it rains every day?' sighed Maria, and together they walked slowly away from the window.

'They are inseparable,' said Isobel to herself, as though the thought had struck her for the first time.

She had consigned them as babies, with dutifulness and relief, to nannies, and now that they were older to Miss Brand. Miss Brand taught them French, piano and sewing. She directed their reading and gave them a grounding in elementary mathematics. She had no doubt taught them more. But Miss Brand, amiable, deferential and quiet in her mistress's presence, had gone to look after an aged cousin for the summer, and her mistress was not sure whether she was relieved or sorry at her absence. She felt vaguely that it was now her duty to penetrate the coterie in which her elder daughters giggled at their own jokes and chattered aimlessly for hours together, the differing elements in their natures unconsciously welded into one unit, so that Sophie was allowed to be domineering and Maria, graciously, to accept all the advantages that Sophie won for them. They probably felt affection for no one but themselves, thought Isobel, and she wished that she was of a more forceful temperament, to be able to break up their tiny universe and rearrange it around all four of them. But the thought of extending herself into their charmed circle and drawing them out of it daunted her.

She had been the eldest of a family which did not begin to expand further until seven or eight years after her birth, and so she had not found herself close to any of the jumble of brothers and sisters that came later. Her youth seemed distant, constrained and shadowy. She could not now even distinguish at which soirée she had been introduced to her husband. Indeed, she thought it probable that he had been introduced to her *as* her husband, for she could not remember meeting anyone who had made her heart beat faster, who had declared their undying love for her, nor any tense moment when she knew that there was a young man closeted with her father in his smoking room, begging for her hand in marriage. There had been a bewilderment of dull Balls and Evenings and Teas, and then – her husband.

Marriage was an important institution, she thought, as she stared mournfully at the sand-dunes. It was important therefore to arrange it with love, and it was one's duty to carry it out with care. Duty was a very comforting word. It explained away every disagreeable thing one had to do. She felt Emma's fingers slide over her own, pulling them away from the windowpane – Emma, the baby of the family, to whom alone she felt close. Emma must be taught duty too, so that her life might be made more bearable.

Lunch restored all their spirits. It was amazing, mused Isobel, the power food had to restore. To dry tears, silence arguments, calm tempers; to draw enemies side by side and make them oblivious of almost everything, except what was on their plates. Even if it was only yesterday's mutton and boiled potatoes.

'It'll be cold, ma'am,' Mrs Freestone had said to her when they had met in the kitchen that morning. She had stood short and squat on the other side of a scrubbed wooden table, like a bull-terrier, four-square against all comers.

'Nothing but cold the first day. I baked some pies and made up some soups against your coming. But till I know your tastes ma'am and what's wanted there din't seem much point us wearin' ourselves out for nothin', so I boiled up some mutton last night.'

'That will do very well,' Isobel had replied.

She had looked at the long, black iron range that stretched half the length of the wall behind Mrs Freestone, at the long-handled tongs, forks and spoons that hung beside it, the copper pans and earthenware dishes stacked upon nearby shelves, and suddenly she had longed to seek out the calm of the drawing room, where she could be alone for a few moments after the commotion of the journey.

'You have all you need?' she ventured, and then thought

13

how foolish that must sound to the old woman. It was like the king of one country asking the king of another whether his troops were in order. But Mrs Freestone merely inclined her head.

'I do, ma'am, I have Minnie here to help me.'

In the shadows of the range moved a tall, gangly girl of about fourteen, round-eyed and red-knuckled, who bobbed a curtsey as though jerked on tight elastic.

'And then there's Mr Budge in the garden.'

'Oh?'

'Yes, ma'am.'

That would be Mr Budge, thought Isobel, looking out through the dining-room windows to where an old man with a bundle of twigs under one arm was slowly crossing the lawn in the direction of a green door set in the wall of the garden. Emma, finishing her mutton, looked up at the same moment and saw him too. She saw how he placed one foot stiffly and carefully in front of the other, how tall he was, and how knobbly and bent, the twigs sticking out sideways from him as though they were extra limbs. She turned to her mother.

'Look, there's a walking apple tree,' she said.

'I think that's Mr Budge.' Isobel smiled back at her.

'Who?' said Maria, twisting round in her chair to see out of the window.

'The gardener,' explained Isobel.

'Where?' snapped Maria.

But Mr Budge was vanishing behind the green door.

'He's gone!' announced Emma, beaming with pride at having seen something Sophie and Maria had missed. And a fight seemed ready to break out again.

'Hush!' whispered Isobel, staring significantly towards the far end of the room. The little girls followed her gaze from chair to empty chair, almost guiltily, as though they expected some reprimand to come from their absent hosts, or out of the sunlight that lay across the polished table-top.

It had been decided during lunch that directly afterwards they should go with Nancy to the beach, and that Isobel would join them later for tea. Isobel sat on alone in the yellow dining room while her daughters went upstairs to change, relishing at last the silence. She was overwhelmed by the sudden desire to do

14

nothing more important than count out her motherhood in little piles of vests and pairs of white socks. To have the furniture rearranged in her bedroom and dressing room. To lay out her brushes and bottles exactly as she wanted them. To take out all her jewels and then put them away again, locking them, as though they were her most secret thoughts, carefully into the small drawer of her dressing case. Just to be alone, all afternoon, among the soft fluttering of her maids.

'Mama!' broke in a voice of unctuous virtuousness. 'Mama, don't you think Emma looks adorable in my blue sash!'

It was Maria, with Emma meekly on one side holding her hand and Sophie on the other. They hovered there in the doorway in a cloud of white muslin, clutching straw boaters with long ribbons and looking, to Isobel, like a vision of perfect innocence and sisterliness. The image of the Family clicking softly into place as one of the ideals of Victorian life, its implications of duty fulfilled, permitted Isobel a feeling of pleasure as worthy as that she anticipated from the heap of small vests. She went with them to the front door, instructing Nancy on the perils of the sea, the delusion of the warmth of a summer's afternoon and the extreme danger of speaking to strangers. All the while she puffed out the fullness of Sophie's sleeves or pulled stray strands of Emma's hair gently back behind her ears.

'Put on your hats.'

She was once more anxious for them to be gone.

Maria marshalled Emma before her like a dowager with her young protégée at a ball, turning to smile indulgently at her mother over the top of Emma's head with a mature complicity that startled Isobel.

'Maria . . . ' whispered Emma with hushed excitement as she reached up to kiss her mother goodbye ' . . . Maria lent me her sash!' And she shut her mouth quickly as though the importance of her words might escape for ever, blushing with pride. Emma was playing the part of a dazzled débutante with delight, clutching her bucket and spade and trotting after Maria up the garden path towards the gate.

Sophie turned in the doorway. 'You don't think,' she said, brushing her hand over her dress, 'that our skirts are too creased?' She spoke almost with a light insolence, looking past her mother rather than at her as though deliberately prolonging their departure by such vanity.

'No, dear,' replied Isobel quickly, 'you all look perfect. Besides,' she added as she stepped back into the cool of the house, 'there will be no one of any consequence to see you.'

Chapter Two

Philip walked slowly along the top of the sand-dunes in the direction of the village, staring intently at the sea, occasionally scanning the beach methodically, up and down, from wave-line to high-tide mark, as though searching for something. From time to time he shifted the wooden box he was holding from one arm to the other. Once or twice he stumbled where the uneven line of the dunes dropped sharply or a tussock of marram grass tripped him. Sometimes he floundered in a sudden patch of soft sand, sinking in over his boots. Finally he halted, out of breath.

He had searched the vast stretch of marsh all day, wandering along pathways between tall reeds, crossing and recrossing the channels of the Dunwich river, walking in the green silence almost all the way to Dunwich and then, sick of seeing nothing but marsh and sky, turning left to climb the sand-dunes and retrace his steps along the wide sweep of bay to Walberswick. The village lay behind him across the marsh, built on a small hill. Where the marsh ended the Walberswick Cut ran, crossed by innumerable little bridges often of no more than a plank of wood. On the other side of the Cut the ground rose into fields that climbed to the high shoulder of the Heath beyond, marked out with hedges and shadowed with dark copses.

It wasn't there. Philip turned slowly back to the sea. And it wasn't there. There was no inspiration to be had *anywhere* today. He flung his painting-box down the sand-dune and slithered after it. They both came to a halt half-way down the slope, embedded in sand. There was sand in his shoes, sand clinging to his woollen socks, sand in the legs of his trousers. It was all most disagreeable. It all added to the irritation of the day, the irritation that was all the worse because it centred on himself, on his complete inability to be inspired. He had wasted the whole of a summer's day, with all its precious light, only to have to admit the possibility that his favourite corner of England might be drying up on him. Shaking the sand from each foot, he planted himself more comfortably in the dune, leaning his elbows on his knees and cupping his chin in his hands as he surveyed the beach below him.

Gradually the anxious expression faded out of his eyes and his face acquired its habitual soft placidity. An almost amused dreaminess seemed to make his whole body inert. His irritation forgotten, and his will put aside, he had become, without being quite aware of it, like a sea-shell hollowed of the creature that normally inhabited it, taken over by some power greater than himself so that he reverberated with the hissing and whispering of the sea below him. His eyes, unblinking in the bright light that flooded them, drew lines between hitherto unconnected objects, making patterns out of these shapes that shifted, blurred, then fused slowly into whole canvases. At length he stretched out his hand to find his painting-box, groping in the sand, fumbling, without altering his gaze, at the catch on the lid.

The part of the beach above which he sat was the area just before the estuary where people generally congregated. Here the village children played, visiting families made encampments out of rugs and picnic baskets, and the shrieks of children paddling at the water's edge mingled with the cries of gulls hunting low over the sea. And it was here, on this particular afternoon, that Philip Steer perched almost out of sight in a hollow in one of the sand-dunes and watched it all, with his sketchbook open on his knees and his pencil hovering and darting over the white page.

It was, to begin with, like any other afternoon. The sea receded a little and the children laughed, dabbling their hands in the water, running after the waves until they broke with a gentle crest of foam and chased the children, screaming happily, back up the beach. A dog barked at the ripples. A tern dropped like a stone into the water and flew up again with a silver fish. Under their parasols, women sat and stared straight at the sea, dreaming of things unknown while their children played. Lone children in sandy, wet worlds of their own making. Children in twos and threes digging for shells, building mansions in the sand, skimming pebbles at an old bottle. Philip's dark eyes stared unblinking, his pencil dipping suddenly every now and then to scribble on the white paper almost without looking at it, like the bobbing oystercatchers with their long delicate beaks, scribbling on the wet sand at the water's edge.

Into that pattern of shifting colour and shadow, some time later, a little skein of figures wove its way in an uneven line. Philip saw them out of the corner of one half-closed eye. He observed how they stumbled in troughs of soft sand above high-water mark, and how their leader led them down on to firm sand, how they bunched together and got separated out again in their erratic procession. Three little girls following a figure in black, walking in that embarrassed way that young girls have when they suddenly find themselves the centre of public attention, setting their heads in the air so that they could hardly see where they were going, marching imperiously forward. As they moved across the sand there was a slight eddying of movement around them, as though their arrival disturbed momentarily the rhythm of life on the afternoon beach. Heads turned, eyes that had seemed shut fast in sleep flicked open, children halted for a second in their play, and the dog at the edge of the sea stopped barking at the waves and turned to bark at the intruders.

The procession turned finally in the direction of the sand-dunes and came straight towards Philip who, motionless in his watcher's invisibility, could see them clearly now. The girl at their head had a droop of crumpled silk flowers on her hat and a look of solid concern on her face. She found a space on the sand that was sufficiently isolated, and they settled themselves into it with a great billowing and spreading of rugs, sitting in a line, self-consciously staring out to sea, their backs to Philip. He leaned forward again over his sketchbook and began drawing the black straw hat; the heavy artlessness of it, the weave that in places had frayed to give, together with the faded flowers, a listless, melancholy air. The same droop showed in the girl's heavy shoulders. He sketched in the neat little boaters that sat primly on either side of her, the striped ribbons on their hats fluttering in the light wind. The two elder girls were remarkable for their hair: long, twisted red-brown curls that shone chestnut in the sun and looked almost fox in the shadows. They had small, oval faces with tight little mouths, unsmiling in their determination to preserve their dignity, mouths that Philip drew with the same curtailed, downward slant that he gave to the corners of their eyes. A slight slant of petulance which

19

would become more marked as they grew older, lines which would soften only in each other's presence, or as a mark of rare favour to some third party. Philip's pencil hesitated. Their little sister sat demurely on the other side of the maid. Her hair under its boater was straight and brown, but Philip felt quite unable to draw her face. His one glimpse of it had shown it to be stunningly full of light. It had reminded him in that instant of a portrait by Reynolds of Nelly O'Brien, the two faces, though twenty years apart, full of light reflected up from white dresses and dark eyes shadowed by wide-brimmed straw hats – eyes that sparkled in the shadows and stared at you with great directness.

Philip sat as still as the stiff figures below him, watching. A dog came prancing up the beach and circled the rugs, waving its tail. The maid ordered it away. But whether her voice lacked conviction, being more used to receiving orders than giving them, or whether it was merely that the dog could understand only the particular Suffolk dialect of that part of the coast, it behaved as though the words were an invitation. It waved its tail faster than before, crouching low over its paws as if a game were about to begin, its lips drawn back over its fangs in a wild grin.

'Go away!' shouted the maid, and shook her fist at it.

The dog darted off towards the sea and came running back almost immediately, its muzzle covered in sand. It barked triumphantly at the maid, and bits of sand fell on to the rug. The girl shouted at it again and leaned forward to brush the sand away. The dog ran off a short distance and sat down on its haunches, panting at them.

Philip sketched in a back view of the tattered black hat confronting a small piebald mongrel with a long lolling tongue. He smiled to himself: poor girl, this might be the very first time she had ever seen the sea, and here it was, an endless wetness with a waste of sand in front that got on everything and in everything, and dogs running wild, to crown it all. She had no doubt had instructions not to let her charges get their feet wet or their frocks dirty. But her charges showed no signs of moving at all. They sat for some time without speaking. Eventually some boys who had been throwing stones at an empty bottle moved away, calling the dog with them. With its departure, tension on the rug relaxed slightly. The two elder girls began to talk to each other in an occasional, desultory sort of way, and their younger sister knelt on the edge of the rug and began to make small castles in the sand.

Philip's attention wandered to a group of village women down near the water's edge. They had two babies with them who crawled from lap to lap while the women talked, their grey dresses and white aprons flat patches of colour against the pale sand. From the mouth of the estuary a fishing-boat sailed out between the two piers. As it entered open sea and caught the breeze its sail filled, and as it passed before the two women they turned and scrambled to their feet, calling out to the men on board, holding up their babies to see the boat. The village lived by the sea, and in the winter storms some of them died by it, too.

Philip thought of the tales Mrs Pearce, his landlady, told him in her tiny parlour at 'The Anchor', about dead men coming home on moonless nights from the sea in the dark hours between midnight and dawn, walking, wet through, from the quay up the road to the village. You never saw them, for there was no one to see, but you heard the sound of their sea-boots in the blackness, squelching on the gravel, and in the morning there would be wet footprints half-way up the road, for they never got past the vicar's house. Or the lights, the little lights that flickered in the marshes on summer nights, that were the souls of drowned fishermen, lost and wandering in the boggy land between the sea and the village, trying to find their way back to those they had loved.

The fishing-boat sped out towards the enticement of the horizon, like a white moth to a candle flame. Philip watched the fishermen's wives as they walked slowly away up the beach towards the village – to wait.

The beach drowsed in the sun and the afternoon wore on. Philip abandoned his sketchbook, lay back in the hollow of soft sand and pulled his hat down over his eyes until only a thin strip of beach was visible, shimmering beyond the shadow of his hat-brim. He dozed, warm and comfortable.

Some time later he woke with a strange feeling of alarm, his eyes still tight shut, so that he woke, as it were, inside his head, as though something had disturbed him from the fragment of a dream, with his senses so thoroughly aroused that he hardly dared open his eyes. His curiosity grew stronger than his alarm, and he peered out from below his hat. Still the dream persisted. Convinced that his eyes played him tricks in the shadows of his hat-brim he tore it off. But the dream didn't end. The woman came on towards him, gliding over the sand, fluttering white muslin, holding a pink silk parasol with a white lace trim, smiling into his eyes, on and on over long seconds, moving without seeming to come any closer. And then, suddenly, she was gone, blotted out of sight by figures which rose up from the beach in front of Philip. He sat up, enraged, and almost leaped to his feet, but thought better of it. Shouts of welcome floated up to the sand-dune where he sat feeling frustrated and self-conscious. He beat the sand off his straw boater and crammed it back on his head. He shook the sand from the legs of his trousers and straightened his cravat with fingers that felt numb with a strange sort of cold. He preened himself anxiously for the time when the apparition would look at him again and yet could not stop himself from shrinking back into the hollow so that he would not be noticed. But he could not take his eyes off her. She had hands that could be clutched, arms that could be clung to; she was real enough almost to over balance in the soft sand and to laugh at the fear of falling. And between the turning and the laughing and the children who ran about in front of her, separating her from him, Philip was sure that every now and then she tilted up her face and glanced at the sand-dune where he sat, looking at him quickly, straight in the eyes. He drew his sketchbook on to his knee and sat awkwardly still. Sometimes he gazed far out to sea and sometimes he watched the little party below him, but always he listened, trying to catch scraps of their conversation: names to repeat to himself in the solitude of his room, the sound of her voice to echo in his head whenever he wanted to hear it. But though sounds did float up to him, he was too far away to hear anything distinctly. There was only the pink silk parasol that seemed to send him semaphore signals as it lay against the woman's shoulder. Twirl and stop. Twirl, twirl, stop. Twirl, twirl, twirl. The afternoon deepened into early evening, the sun glinting obliquely against every grain of sand, turning them gold and making them sparkle in the warm light. The little family sat on until they were almost the last on the beach, and then they rose suddenly, all together. The parasol was furled against the evening breeze, the youngest child gathered up her bucket and spade, the woman stood for a moment as though quite alone and stared out to sea. Then they trailed in a long line across the wide beach in the direction of the quay, without a backward glance at either the maid shaking sand out of the rugs, or Philip sitting alone on the sand-dune.

When he arrived back at 'The Anchor', Mrs Pearce was standing in the doorway pulling dead flowers from the rosebush that grew rampant over the wall and hung down over the doorway of the inn, snapping their stems between finger and thumb. An old man sat near her, in shirtsleeves and a moleskin waistcoat, a battered hat on his head and a mug of ale on his knees, laughing toothlessly at something the landlady was saying. She turned as Philip approached to throw a handful of withered roses into a basket at her feet, smiling broadly.

'We're late this evening, Mr Steer!' she cried, and her sharp bar-room eyes missed nothing: the blush, the tousledness, the altogether newness of the boy who stood before her, so ill at ease on such an ordinary evening, clutching his painting-box as though it contained his most prized and private possessions. She moved forward a step so that she blocked the doorway, and pulled her shawl more closely around her shoulders, smiling provocatively at Philip's discomfort. The old man sucked at his ale, his little eyes gleaming over the top of his mug.

'Why Mr Steer, you'll paint the eyes right out of your head! T'ain't so warm out on them dunes when the heat of the day's gone, though the sun do shine half the night. See somethin' pretty, did you, for your picture?'

Philip smiled wanly and waved his hand dismissively in the air, more to clear away the image of the pink silk parasol and the beautiful face beneath from Mrs Pearce's inquisitive grin than to signify the modesty of his painting achievements – more to wave away the immobile bulk of his landlady so that he could escape into the dark hallway of the inn and make his way quickly to the privacy of his room on the first floor. In the silence the old man looked from one to the other expectantly, his mouth half open.

'Just some sketching,' muttered Philip.

'Ah,' replied Mrs Pearce, and nodded.

Philip nodded back at her, slowly, hoping thereby to end matters. And the old man, as though hypnotised, nodded too, over his mug of ale, with a slightly perplexed expression. They were like strangers in some oriental land, who meet without a common language, nodding and smiling, uttering soft sounds to express their goodwill.

'This is Walter,' announced Mrs Pearce, as though letting go one quarry only to seize another. 'Mr Smytheson's gardener.'

'Oh,' said Philip, ' . . . indeed?'

'Ar,' said the old man, and took another swig of his ale.

'Walter says,' continued Mrs Pearce, with the quick delighted speech of a gossip relaying her information to a new listener, 'Mr Smytheson's come downstairs this morning for the very first time. Didn't he, Walter? Took 'im half an hour. But he made it. Spent all day lying on a sofa in the morning room – Walter saw him through the window!'

'I'd better go and pay my respects,' said Philip.

'You must indeed, sir. Them old bones of his, surviving that accident, 'tis a miracle.' She paused, but Philip was unforthcoming. 'You should go tomorrow.'

Philip saw the inquisitorial gleam again in her eyes. If she expected him to demur on account of some other appointment, he would disappoint her.

'I shall call on him first thing,' he replied, pushed past her into the sanctuary of the hallway and fled to his room.

If getting past Mrs Pearce and through the door of 'The Anchor' had felt like gaining sanctuary, Philip expected the closing of the bedroom door to confer on him utter peace. But, of course, it did not. He sank down on the bed, stood his painting-box neatly by its side and waited for the beating of his heart to subside and the calmness of the room to subdue his confused feelings. He sat and waited for the room to come to his aid. But nothing happened. The room didn't even seem aware that he was in it. The mirror over the washstand in the far corner went on darkly reflecting the wall opposite and the religious text that hung over his bed. The table beneath the window, covered with painting and writing materials, seemed absorbed in its own mahogany ponderousness. The brushes laid out on the chest of drawers were as uncommunicative as hedgehogs and dust danced languorously in a shaft of evening sunlight that fell on the rug beside his bed as though entirely unobserved.

What he now perceived as the deliberate silence of the room, far from calming him, made him more agitated than ever. Now that the door was shut he wanted it open. Now that he was alone he wanted to be among people. Now that all the questions could race in safety round his head without discovery he wanted to spill them out before people who might know the answers. He thought of going down into the taproom of the inn, to the old men with their long clay pipes and their interminable pint pots, and recoiled again into his habitual shyness. He could not talk to them, and they could not talk to him. He could not ask them who she was, or where she was, or whether she was sister, aunt or cousin to the little girls on the beach. Or – something else.

He got up from the bed and paced round and round the room, stopping occasionally in front of the door as though he wanted to fling it open, while all the time he worried at the new obsessions of images, questions, longings and superstitions, gnawing them, like a dog at a bone, into a shape accessible to his desire. It took him quite some time, as the exercise was new to him, and by the time he had accomplished it and felt all the edges of truth rubbed away and the glowing image of the woman in white muslin nestled comfortably and unshakably in his heart, so that he felt it beat with a new pride and an added reverberation of responsibility, it had grown quite late. The room behind him was almost in darkness, and outside his window, beyond the cornfields and marshes towards Dunwich, the line of sand-dunes was black against the apricot light that flooded the evening sky. Suddenly he longed for Sickert's bantering idiocy, or Shannon, or any of them. To have them all there, downstairs, in the snug, with supper and wine. To surround himself with their lightheartedness, their common-sense and their nonsense and the protection of their camaraderie against such dreams as these. As these white arms that reached up and up as though from the deepest lake, closed his eyes, twined themselves around his neck and leant his head back against the window recess, drifting with him into such realms of sensation as he had never known existed.

Chapter Three

When he woke the next day, long fingers of grey cloud splashed across the sky from the direction of Dunwich, lying like spreading stains above the marsh. Everything else sparkled with the clarity of morning as though the whole village, clean and sleepy, hung in a dewdrop. Even the sea lay mirror-clear, deceiving itself with its own image.

Philip bustled about the room, dressing and packing for the day's painting excursion.

'It's going to rain,' he said to himself, with a feeling of dread, quite undeterred by the blueness of the sky. He was troubled not only by symptoms of the condition of the weather (for a healthy young man he was obsessed by the fear of getting his feet wet) but also by symptoms of his own altered state, of which he became embarrassedly aware. He was, as a rule, a very calm, methodical young man, quiet, a little set, perhaps, in his habits for one so young, but that did help the externals to be taken care of in such a way as to leave his thoughts or, more accurately, his energies, free for painting. But this morning – and as the thought came to him he made himself stand still for a second and try to control the quivering that shook his body – he was darting around his room like a dragonfly. Normally he dressed slowly and carefully in a logical procession from vest to cravat. Today he had begun dressing, caught sight of his painting-box open on the table, sprinted over to it and begun to cram instruments inside, pushing the pencils where the paintbrushes should have gone, crushing yesterday's paint-streaked rag on top of everything instead of tearing off a clean piece from the old sheet which lay folded on the chair. Then, suddenly, deciding the weather would turn wet, he had abandoned his packing and gone scurrying to the far side of the room to forage for his galoshes and umbrella. And he didn't even have his socks on. He stood on the rug, trembling, a little afraid of this 'seizure', and looking down realised that he didn't have his trousers on either. He sat heavily on the bed. Above the buzzing in his head, he could hear the vast pounding of his heart.

What did it mean? Why was he doing this? What was he rushing about for? He never rushed. Besides, this was Walberswick, not London. He had no appointments here, no lecture to attend, no vernissage to be late for, no engineered introduction by some kind friend to forget. No one to see, no one that he knew he was going to see – for certain. He felt his heart tighten, and the fear of it tingle in a way that, new and alarming though it was, he was beginning to like. He thought of chance meetings. And marvelled at how quiet the room seemed to grow. A little strip of white muslin blew on some sea-wind into a corner of his mind and he felt all the muscles in his shoulders go slack and melt and swirl. He opened his eyes and the rushing feeling began again. He must get dressed. And pack. Because . . . He stood in the middle of the room, perplexed, and longed for some reason to save him from all this. Then he laughed. 'Of course!' Of course, there was both reason and purpose to the day – he was going to see Smytheson this morning. That was it. He pulled on his trousers and buttoned them up.

'I'm going to see poor old Smytheson,' he muttered to himself as he wriggled his feet into his boots and tied up the laces. 'Poor chap,' he continued, putting together the rest of his painting things, talking to himself a little breathlessly and whisperingly, as one does to keep ghosts at bay. 'Cheer him up a bit.' And clutching umbrella, canvas stool, painting-box and woollen scarf, he hurled himself through the door, banging it shut behind him and clattering down the wooden stairs.

Mrs Pearce had been hovering for some hours, and when she heard the commotion she darted out of her parlour and neatly collided with Philip in the hall.

'Sleep well, did we, Mr Steer?'

'Thank you,' blushed Philip, courteously inclining his head and at the same time pushing past her towards the sunlight beyond the open front door.

'We're later than usual . . . '

'Lovely day,' he called from the safety of the inn yard, bravely putting his head back into the dark hall to add, 'Just off to see Mr Smytheson, before I go painting!' And was gone.

Mrs Pearce stamped off to the kitchen.

'Well, my young fighting cock!' she muttered angrily.

The room was empty, save for an old hag in the corner, bent over a tub of potatoes, peeling them with painful slowness.

'Bring me some tea, Agnes!' shouted Mrs Pearce from the doorway. Then she stamped back to the parlour and slammed the door behind her. Agnes straightened her bent back, rested her wet hands on her knees and spat into the potatoes.

Horace Smytheson lived at the other end of the village, next to the church, almost the last building on the high road before it swept round a spinney of trees and disappeared into the rough and tumble of the heath. It was a large house, protectively masked by a great variety of tall, dark trees, so that one guessed at its size and its character from the length of wall that ran alongside the road, the partial view of gables and corners, and the curiously shaped windows visible through the trees. He lived there alone save for his bull terrier, Mug, and a couple called Arthur, who looked after him.

On this particular June morning, his world was only just settling back into its habitual comfort, after having been literally turned upside down, indeed almost obliterated, by a driving accident. When Philip arrived at the front door he was met by Mrs Arthur.

'Lovely day, Mr Steer,' she said politely, ushering him into the hall.

'It's going to rain,' replied Philip as he unwound his scarf, peeled off his galoshes and divested himself of his overcoat. Mug sniffed at the growing pile of strange objects and pattered after the visitor, his claws sliding on the polished floor.

'In the study, Mr Steer.'

'Ah, yes,' exclaimed Philip and strode after her. He was rather warm and wondered if it was continued agitation, or just the weather. His hair felt sticky on his forehead, and he brushed it back with a shaky hand. Mrs Arthur opened the study door and Philip, stepping forward, drew in his breath sharply, feeling almost as if he were going to faint. The room was stiflingly hot. Red wallpaper, red velvet curtains and a red Turkey carpet on the floor all reflected the glow of a tiny fire built in the grate.

Mr Smytheson lay on a horse-hair sofa, apparently covered in sheets of newspaper.

'Philip, my dear boy! This is very good of you, very civil. Do sit down. Anywhere you please, make yourself at home.'

The only other pieces of furniture in the room were a vast kneehole desk pushed against the window and a round-backed swivel chair before it into which Philip dropped, swinging it from side to side to create a slight draught of air in the over-heated room. The old man rustled the sheets of newspaper, drawing them, like a blanket, up to his chin.

'Lookin' well, my boy, lookin' well. Ah, the flush of youth. Look like you've been stridin' about.' He shook his head pensively. 'I was a walkin' man myself, Philip, when I was young. Gun in my hand, dog at my heels. Sir Ralph Blunden's father kept a good shoot in those days. It would be up over the moor and down through Tinkers' Covert, flushin' the birds out over the marsh. Or on over the Top, across the road and along the Mile. Didn't have Mug in those days,' he chortled. 'No.' He screwed his eyes up as if looking far back into the past. 'I used to have a bitch. Best out of a whole succession of bitches. A bitch out of a distant cousin's dog, mouth like velvet, and obedient! You'd draw breath and she'd lift her head and prick up her ears. She'd know before you saw the bird fall that you'd made a hit; she'd be off from your heel, straight as a knife . . . ' and the old man flung out his arm to demonstrate.

'Oh, lor'!' he yelped, his face suddenly scarlet with pain. 'Phew!' he breathed, nursing the arm to his side with his other hand. 'I keep on forgettin' these darned ribs.'

Philip had leapt to his feet at the first cry, and now hovered by the bell-pull, unsure whether he should summon Mrs Arthur.

'Sit down, my boy, sit down. Don't call Mrs Arthur, she'll have me back in bed in a trice. She follows me around the house with fires as it is. Fires, in the middle of June! I'm walkin', though, Philip, I'm walkin'.'

Philip subsided in his chair. 'I confess when I first heard of your fall, I feared . . . '

He stopped in confusion. His emotions were so wildly to the fore of everything else he felt almost unable to speak without exposing them. He was acutely embarrassed to be so out of control in front of the old man, but Smytheson, with tact and affection, broke in.

'So did I, dear boy, so did I.'

'. . . and now to hear that you are walking again is wonderful.'

The old man nodded. 'You shall accompany me on my first stroll through the village. In ten days' time – I have a wager with my doctor and you shall help me win it.'

Philip grinned. 'I should be delighted.'

'That's settled.' Smytheson beamed. 'But you know what's not settled, Philip, for the legal man in me who likes there to be a nice, clear-cut case with one side and another and a decision and a rollin'-up and a tyin' with pink ribbon. For the detective in me – for you know we solicitors, while we perforce must take on trust every word our client says, must do a bit of our own devillin' and askin' of questions and lookin' for answers – well, for the detective in me my accident don't make sense at all! That's what I can't abide. There's a reason for everythin' in the law-books. But there's no reason for this accident, ferret about in my head for it though I might.'

'Reason?' echoed Philip, who felt at that moment very far indeed from such a state of being and wasn't sure that he would ever make his return. 'I thought your horse reared?'

'Yes, but why?'

'Well, horses do jump about a bit,' replied Philip with a shudder, 'if something scares them.'

'Nothin' much scares my old mare – placid as a mill-pond and almost as old as I am. The only thing she can't abide is pigs. Merest whiff of 'em and she lays her ears back. There we were, drivin' along, empty heath silent in the sunshine, not a cloud in the sky, not a person in sight, not a pig for miles . . . '

The old man talked on and Philip's mind began to wander. The semaphore of the pink parasol began to flutter like a butterfly in his head, like the butterflies that fluttered among the pink thrift flowers along the sand-dunes. She might be taking a walk at this very moment. And he might not be there to see her. He must leave. The old man talked on, delighted to have an audience.

'. . . my old bones on the back of a farm cart. All I can say is thank God it happened in England and not in Paris . . . '

Philip writhed in his chair in despair at his inability to depart.

'Yes, indeed,' nodded Smytheson, mistaking Philip's anguish. He rattled the sheets of newsprint that covered his chest. 'You know the disaster at the Paris Opéra when all those people were crushed and burned to death, well, they're havin' to set guard over the corpses, not just against theft of the dead people's jewels, but of their very bones. Their very bones, Philip, think of it! They sell them to each other, dastardly French. Nasty, pasty-faced lot.'

Horace Smytheson subsided, nodding, into the pages of that morning's *Times*, preparing to recount further disasters. Philip envisioned being detained for another hour, while the whole paper was read to him.

'I must go,' he announced, standing up quickly, 'to catch the light.'

Halfway along the High Street stood a windmill, built on the shoulder of a vast cornfield, each of its sails set at a different angle to catch every wind that blew. Beside it was a bedraggled line of pines, and between the trees and the windmill a footpath led away from the village around the edge of the field, down into the marsh. It was to this footpath that Philip escaped soon after leaving Smytheson's house. He had no sooner achieved his object of freeing himself, of putting himself in the path of the woman with the parasol, than he became terrified that he might actually meet her, and though not a soul seemed to be about as he walked down the High Street he felt himself to be an obvious and ridiculous figure. Seeing the opening of the path, he fled down it in relief.

Below him lay the marsh, and beyond it the sea. Around him the corn rustled in the heavy stillness. The fingers of cloud he had noticed earlier had grown into a vast hand that now almost covered the marsh. Below the cloud the sun shone livid, highlighting the crests of foam to a brilliant white on the dark sea, as the sky grew more and more threatening.

He stared down into the marsh, fascinated, watching the life go out of it as the cloud crept over. An inch of reed would be all manner of greens, browns, touches of ochre and streaks of blue as it bent and waved in the wind, and then, a moment later, as the shadow of the cloud moved forward over that inch of land, it would be – dead. Almost monochrome in the absence of light. Dull as all its neighbours, bending meekly in an anonymous mass. It was light, light that was the most important thing. If one could paint in light, then every colour would resonate, and have value, in exactly the way and proportion that it did in reality.

He began to walk down the footpath that divided the wheatfield, matching his pace to the deliberations in his mind. This must be the solution to the problem of painting not only what one saw but what one felt – heat, rain, snow, mist, grey November cold – everything. Not by painting only the final effects of those states of atmosphere, the colours, but by going right back to first principles: by sucking up Nature herself and issuing forth light. In the excitement of it, Philip felt again the ache to achieve the almost impossible task. To discover the secret of light would be like holding the key to everything in one's hand. He saw in his mind his studio in Tite Street and himself in front of a canvas; canvas after canvas, pushing himself on with a kind of bruised stubbornness that had scarcely a hair's breadth of strength left in it, confronting an unfinished, unfinishable picture that refused to come together. When one had no skill left, no knowledge one had not tried, one reached on bodyless into a kind of no-man's land, painting on in an unconscious daze, no longer in control of what one was doing. Then, drained, standing back from the canvas to find it was as close as one had yet come to perfection. The elation; the prickling of tears of utter exhaustion; the release with honour from the tyranny of the studio; the way in which his legs almost trembled as he walked, still in a slight trance, down the stairs. The strange flatness of the world outside. What power could be his if he could find the solution. Here, he could sit outside day after day surrounded by light, and paint and paint until he discovered its secret, abandoning himself to paint and sunlight all summer long, as another man might abandon himself to wine.

He let his free hand trail across the surface of the field, and the tips of the stalks tickled his palm. Around him the corn was as high as his waist, flecked with green and yellow. It was like wading through water. As the summer wore on it would become heavy and dry, its head drooping as July blazed into August, as though it became aware of its approaching death. The long, slow swelling of the year and the explosion into fruition. Did fruition always end in a kind of death? Was it the seeking that kept us alive? Was it a cruel promise of fulfilment that whispered us awake? Were we teased into life? Were the prizes, when we opened them, just packets of disillusion? Should he draw back into the comfortable seclusion of being unknown? He wavered for a moment, standing there in the cornfield with all of summer buzzing around him. He felt his heart begin to thud wildly, like the drumming heels of a terrified rabbit, before the spectre of his indecision. No. No, he could not turn back. He was involved. He was intrigued, engaged, embroiled. And, he smiled to himself, besides, he was in love. As he allowed his mind to say these words, he felt his heart at last subside, as though a danger had passed. He felt his face flush with pleasure and, in the shyness of admitting such a thing, even to himself, he bent his head to the ground. Down to the busy world, that scuttled on, oblivious of his great joy, amid the tangles of dry grass and bare earth and mountainous pebbles. Where ants, beetles and spiders scurried from the protection of one leaf to another, dragging their trophies behind them.

Suddenly, into that enchanted world there burst the sound of voices. Philip stared around him wildly, but the field was empty. He was by now almost at its far edge, where there was a gap in the hedge leading down to the marsh, and he crept forward to peer through. As he got closer, he could distinguish a voice, tinkling on like a sheep's bell, a light, childish monotone that scarcely paused for breath. He inched slowly forward and peered through the hawthorn prickles. As he did so, broken ends of straw and a bunch of faded poppies suddenly bobbed up in front of him, a face thrust itself into his and a woman screamed.

Down on the marsh, Emma emerged, a tiny, demure figure, from a jungle of reeds, talking loudly to Dolly whom she imagined to be just in front of her. The narrow track which she followed now led on to one of the many plank bridges which spanned Walberswick Cut on its progress through the marsh. Emma placed one neat foot carefully in front of the other, engrossed in the importance of not overbalancing, staring down

33

at the twinkling of her black-booted toes and below them at the water as it ran dark under the bridge and clear again in the sunlight. She wondered whether there might not be a dragon under the bridge and went extra carefully just in case. Ahead of her, Dolly floundered up the bank of earth towards a gap in a long hedge which skirted the edges of the fields as they rose steeply away from the marsh. Emma heard her slithering and cursing. And then she heard her scream. She looked up quickly. Outlined against the cornfield and the sky was Dolly, her arms waving wildly, and a man clutching her by the shoulders. It was impossible for the moment to tell whether he was pulling her up the bank or pushing her down. Emma stared at the struggling couple more with curiosity than alarm. She saw Dolly finally detach herself from the stranger's arms and reach the safety of the footpath, her hat askew and her face very red, but otherwise unharmed. Indeed, for all the commotion she had made, the adventure seemed not to have frightened her at all, for she tottered towards the edge of the bank, clutching her hat with one hand and stretching the other down to Emma. The stranger beside her leaned forward too, as though to help, staring at her intently.

'Oh, Miss Emma,' cried Dolly breathlessly, 'Miss Emma, do take care!'

Philip had recognised Dolly as his model from the previous summer. Now he saw that Emma was the little girl from the beach party of the day before. The thought flashed through his head that between them they could tell him everything he wanted to know.

'Don't fuss, Dolly!' shouted Emma from the bottom of the bank, determined not to be thought a baby in front of the stranger. She began to climb, pulling herself up by tufts of grass and overhanging hawthorn twigs.

'Mind your dress!' shrieked the maid.

'Allow me,' said Philip and reached his arm down to her. Emma stretched out her hand to his, feeling very grand and daring and hoping she would not, having to relinquish the safety of the grass, slither back down to the bottom again. She felt herself, instead, pulled through the air to stand beside him on the path. They all three looked down into the empty marsh. It had now completely lost its greenness and looked very dark.

'Come on, Miss Emma,' said Dolly anxiously, 'let's get you home before them clouds break. Mr Steer, you i'nt goin' off paintin'! There's weather comin' ain't fit for a dog.'

'Yes,' muttered Philip. He bent to hide the confusion he felt at Emma's departure and began to pick up his things. 'Yes, I thought I would . . . '

'Is that what you've got in your box – paints?' asked Emma.

'Yes.'

'I've got a paint-box at home, but it isn't nearly that big.'

'Well, I have a lot of things in it.' He wondered fleetingly why he did carry so much around with him. To justify himself he added, 'I'm here for the summer to paint, so I have to make sure I have everything with me.'

'We're here for the summer, too!' cried Emma. 'Right up to September. We're living in Quay House, almost on the beach!'

'Then I look forward to the pleasure of meeting you,' he hesitated, 'and your family, again.'

He raised his hat. Emma did a wobbly curtsey and then rushed for the safety of Dolly's hand. Having gained it, she turned and smiled coquettishly.

'Will you paint my picture?'

'I should be honoured,' replied Philip.

'Come *on*, Miss,' repeated Dolly. 'Goodbye, Mr Steer, sir.'

Instead of Emma, Philip imagined the woman with the parasol captive in front of his canvas. He turned quickly away and slid in a rush down the bank, took the plank bridge at a run and ended up in the seclusion of the reeds, breathless and elated. Why, he virtually had an entry to their house! He felt like hurling paints and umbrella up in the air and shouting for glee. Instead, he turned and watched the little figures struggling up the hill to the village. Too far away now for him to hear how Emma bombarded Dolly with questions about him and hung upon every word of her replies to boast about afterwards to her sisters.

The thought of painting the woman with the parasol began to obsess Philip. It became an excuse for his growing obsession with the woman herself. *She* would provide the inspiration that had otherwise been lacking in the familiar landscape. To meet her, therefore, became of growing urgency; it was also a prospect that filled him with alarm, the kind of alarm which is both fear and delight – and utterly compelling. He reasoned that he should contrive to meet her with the little girl, for then he would have an immediate introduction to her. He now knew where they were staying and could guess that they would be most likely to frequent either the quay or the beach, there being little else of note in the village.

For the next few days, he too haunted these places. Each day he would emerge from 'The Anchor', carrying his painting things, and walk down Quay Road, past their house (which he would hardly dare look at) to the harbour, where he would inspect the drying fishing-nets, or gaze at the slow windings of the chain ferry as it went back and forth across the river. Sometimes he would try to sketch. Always he would feel anxious, turning often towards the road to see whether they came, wondering whether they might have got to the beach without his noticing them. Finally, gathering up his things with as much nonchalance as possible, he would make his way to the shore. Here he would walk along the water's edge to assure himself they were not on the sands, climb up into the dunes to wait for them and then wander off into the marsh. In these first days, he did indeed see Emma several times, but never in the company of the woman with the parasol.

It had been Philip's custom to spend all day on sketching trips in the countryside around the village, but now, like some winter-starved bird, hungry for a sight of the woman, he was driven in from the marshes and fields. He started to return to 'The Anchor' in the middle of the day for lunch, hoping that in this way he doubled the chance of being in the same part of the village at the same time as his quarry. He left at a different time each morning and returned to the inn at a different time each afternoon. He began to be successful. The first time he saw her, he had just arrived at the top of Quay Road to descend to the beach, and there she was, turning out of the gate of Quay House with a maid. They walked towards the harbour and Philip followed, magnetised. At the first of the fishermen's huts, as they vanished out of sight to reappear on the bridge, he came to his senses, lost courage, turned and walked quickly back up the road into the safety of the cornfields, where he sat, drawing her from memory all afternoon.

Thus he learned the pattern of her days and made them his. He made 'appointments' with her, which invariably they both kept. His frenzy and the tickling fear which this passion aroused gave way often to a kind of calm. He lived now by his watch in a way he had never done before, disrupting his painting to hurry back to the village to catch a glimpse of her. Strangely, he rarely saw her with Emma. On the two occasions he did, he was so suddenly gripped with shyness and concern for the ridiculousness of his passion that he could not bring himself to speak to them, but stayed, frozen, where he was, at a safe distance. His sketchbook had by now become more like a schoolboy's notebook than that of a serious artist, the margins crowded with thumbnail sketches of the woman with the parasol, until Philip hardly knew whether he really remembered the minute details of her clothes and expressions, or whether she was just a fantasy.

On one of his painting trips into the marsh, he sat, as usual, day-dreaming over his pencil when he suddenly realised that the light around him was draining away. The clouds had become so heavy overhead that the reeds seemed almost black; they rustled together like people whispering in a nightmare as the wind gusted and then dropped. He was struck by an eerie sense of claustrophobia. Everything was silent – a waiting silence, like a bubble about to burst. In front of him the sand-dunes were a thick smudge against the black clouds. Far to the right was the village, accessible only by certain paths through boggy ground. Philip was filled with a kind of panic. The familiarity of the Town Salts was quite gone; even the reed warblers and gulls were hushed and out of sight. He started to run towards the sand-dunes, seeking the open safety of the beach, and as soon as he ran he became convinced that he was being chased. He slithered on the narrow paths and panted up the soft slopes of the dunes. At the top he paused for a second and looked over his shoulder in terror, but nothing moved in the marshes. He ran down to the beach seeking firmer sand. The sea, too, was black, except way out on the horizon where it shimmered silver as though the sun was shining in another land. The low swell eased its way over the water and broke without a sound on the shore.

Philip turned and began running towards the estuary. As he did so the rain began. Single drops at first, with a vehement heaviness, like accusing fingers, landed on his head and shoulders. They fell like ink blots into the sand, leaving a splattered mark on the pale surface, and dropped into the sea like small stones. Ploughing through the sand, Philip could hear the rain fall faster and faster, its pace outstripping his own until he felt, despite all his efforts, helpless against the powers of the elements set against him. By the time he reached the quay, the rain was a solid sheet and he could hear thunder rumbling away to his left. Gasping for breath and cursing his foolhardiness at ever having set out at all in such uncertain weather, he struggled up the road and finally arrived at 'The Anchor'.

He spent the rest of the afternoon in his room, sitting huddled in blankets with his feet in a mustard bath. Rain kept hissing down the chimney, and the wind blew first from this quarter, so that soot fluttered out on to the hearth, then from that, making the windows rattle. He stared out at the rain and thought miserably of the chill he would no doubt develop; from time to time he felt his forehead and cleared his throat to see whether it had not already arrived. He felt acutely depressed at the thought of anything disrupting his painting schedule, especially anything that might take as unforeseeably long as an illness. It produced in him a feeling of frustration which was as close to anger as he ever got, and in which he had a sudden inkling of the possible meaninglessness of life. For he could not bear to imagine life without painting. He was always in the middle of painting or waiting to paint, waiting for a model or planning a sketching trip. If anything occurred outside his control to hinder these essential states of mind, he became completely put out, driven from his serenity into a waste land where the fear that this unaccustomed lack of purpose aroused only destroyed further the calm that his creativity needed in order to function. It was all a vicious circle, which upset him profoundly. He peered mournfully at the streaming windows, and wished he had packed his bottle of Collis Browne's Chloro-dyne.

When, an hour later, Mrs Pearce knocked on his door with a cup of steaming beef tea, he was wistfully grateful.

''Tis the real thing, Mr Steer, do you more good than any of them shop Essences.'

Philip held the cup between both hands.

'Brand's is really very good,' he murmured. 'They do an Essence of Turtle which is quite delicious.'

'Turtle!' snorted Mrs Pearce. 'And where do they get them, may I ask. There ain't no turtles on English shores. Nobody I ever knew got well off no turtle!'

'I think I should take only the lightest of suppers,' said Philip, 'and have it in my room.'

'Feed a cold, Mr Steer! And chase it away with a little light company.'

Philip shook his head slowly. The idea of anything breaking in on his delicately balanced state of health horrified him.

'I'll come up again at supper-time and see if you won't change your mind.'

Down in her kitchen, Mrs Pearce felt all of a twitter with strangely mixed emotions.

'He's sitting up there, convinced he's dying from the wetting he got and raving like a child in a fever about turtles!' She went and banged aimlessly about among the jars of preserve in her larder. 'What he needs is a mother or a wife,' she muttered. 'Sitting up there on his own, wrapped up in blankets in the middle of summer, his little face peering out at that rain . . . '

By evening the rain had stopped. Mrs Pearce announced to Philip that the storm had gone away over the sea, as though he were a child waking from a bad dream, and fancied that he brightened visibly. But he refused to come downstairs, taking himself off to bed as soon as his supper was cleared away. He lay there in a state of uneasiness that was not pure concern for his health, feeling that the afternoon's episode had cast a blight on the whole summer's prospects. The unnatural darkness and the feeling of hushed fear that had been all around him in the marsh haunted him still. He thought of the meeting with the unknown woman that he had missed and saw again the group on the beach, falling asleep with the image of a broad-brimmed hat and all the sunlight of a summer's afternoon reflected in the beautiful face beneath.

Chapter Four

Late that night, when all the village slept, far out to sea the tide turned upon itself and rushed towards the land. In the dark mouth of the estuary, streaked silver by clouds torn across the moon, the fishing-boats felt the first tremor of the swell and swung creaking in unison to turn in obeisance on their anchor chains. The gulls stirred slightly in their sleep at the top of the masts and buried their heads more deeply into their wing feathers. And, racing in with the tide, its energy replenished ten times over, came the storm. It pushed the already eager waves before it into mountains of water that thundered on to the beach, crashing higher and higher against the sand-dunes and vying with the thunderclaps overhead. It tore at the chains that tethered the fishing-boats and tossed them wildly on long, shuddering waves, hurling those nearest the quay against the wooden piers. Wide, white flashes of lightning lit up the whole area and the rain lashed at the green corn in the fields and the reeds on the Town Salts as though trying to tear them out by the very roots. Rainwater streamed down every incline and swept through most of the hovels in the village. It ran down the road to the quay and poured into the already brimming estuary. Towards dawn, the storm tired of its own devastation and retreated back over the sea, whence it had come.

Philip slept fitfully during the night, the crashing overhead merging with the pandemonium of his dreams. He woke late and lay there, waiting to discover symptoms of chill or fever; finding none, he climbed out of bed to see what damage the storm had done. He was amazed, on drawing his curtains, to see blue sky and sunshine. Unaccountably, his spirits soared. Everything sparkled, light reflecting back out of the pools of water that lay everywhere.

As he walked down to the harbour, the ground around him steamed in the sunshine, trees dripped, leaves and twigs were everywhere. Fistfuls of thatch hung from the roofs of the cottages as though a giant had torn them out in his rage.

Further on, near the entrance to the common, a sapling had been uprooted and lay broken in the road. Philip kicked it aside. The village and the marsh lay still in the sunlight as though exhausted. Over it all hung the treacherous innocence of blue sky.

When he got closer to the quay, Philip saw that all the village seemed to be gathered there. Like any crowd that gathers to witness the aftermath of some drama, the crowd that milled around the Hard felt the ordinariness of their lives touched by momentary excitement, as though the emotional and physical impact of an event, in the explosion of its happening, sets up shock-waves which reverberate in that place and temporarily electrify all who come within range.

Among the groups of villagers, Philip could make out the vicar and the nodding bonnets of the vicar's wife and the two Miss Mayhews. He saw Mr Smytheson's housekeeper talking to a woman in black nursing a baby, and caught sight of Dolly Brown near the water's edge with a diminutive straw-hatted figure beside her. As he drew nearer, Philip saw that most of the men were clustered around a fishing-boat that was lying on its side. Its mast was splintered in several places and it was surrounded by a tangle of ropes. The men stared at it, moving little and hardly speaking, as though the strange phenomenon of a boat on dry land perplexed them all.

The vicar came forward to greet Philip, his eyes sparkling with excitement.

'My dear boy, my dear boy! What do you think? You've seen it? This poor community of souls — I thank God none of them was lost.' Taking hold of Philip's arm, he steered him through the groups of people. 'The wildness of the storm,' he shook his head. 'The raging of the wind. It was worse in Hungary, you know, yesterday. Forty thousand acres submerged!' He put his head close to Philip's and gripped his arm even tighter: 'They can't tell how many dead!' he added, almost in a whisper.

He halted Philip as they came level with the stranded boat. The men were just bending to pick up the ropes.

'Poor souls,' whispered Reverend Rount in Philip's ear. 'Up since dawn and before. I fancied I heard sea-boots running past my house all night.' He paused, and then, 'See that boat?'

41

Philip nodded. 'There were two. See how the top of one of the masts has torn a hole in the side of that hut? See! Wonder it wasn't carried away by the same waves that lifted these creatures up on to the Hard. The other boat was down there, sideways, thrown up on the shingle below these huts to the right. Front caved in on a bollard. Holes all down the side. Driven against stakes, you know, lower down.'

Still clutching Philip's arm and turning this way and that, pouring new disasters in his ear and pushing through the crowd as though ushering an important guest to a front seat at a spectacle, Reverend Rount emerged at the water's edge. Behind the cluster of boats drawn up on the Hard for safety was a wreck-strewn shingle beach and six or seven black tarred huts on stilts. One had its roof blown away, another its door torn off by the hinges and a fishing-net thumping and flapping, entangled on the wooden pinnacle over the gaping doorway. Little boys ran everywhere, as excited by the wreckage as the vicar, scavenging with the old men among the flotsam of the storm. On opposite sides of the quay, Mrs Rount and Mrs Arthur moved among the fishermen's wives and, with the insinuation of assistance and sympathetic cluckings and shakings of the head, elicited every detail they could. They turned through the rubble of these women's lives, pouncing on gleams of starvation, digging for smashed fragments of wrecked boats and lost tackle, hoarding their finds to pore over again in the warm comfort of their houses, protected from the vagaries of such storms by thick walls and positions of security within society.

But it was none of these women that held Philip's interest. It was a woman for whom Philip had looked the moment he arrived on the quay. Not finding her, he had glanced repeatedly over his shoulder, scanning the road. He had hoped, without quite being aware of his longing, that she would have been among the crowd. Perhaps she stayed away out of delicacy, out of the wish not to appear, as a stranger, to pry. All of a sudden there was a grating sound and a corresponding flurry among the onlookers as the men around the stranded boat pulled on the ropes and began hauling it towards the water. People stumbled backwards out of their way, and Philip took advantage of the confusion to move forward so that he stood next to Dolly and the little girl, who were also watching the refloating of the boat.

'Good morning, Dolly, Miss Emma.' Philip raised his cap. Dolly blushed and made as if to move away. But the little girl looked up at him and smiled.

'Isn't it exciting!' she said, her eyes shining.

'Do you find it so?' He grinned down at her enthusiastic face. 'Weren't you frightened by all the thunder and lightning in the night?'

'Oh, yes! I was so frightened at first that I hid under the bedclothes, it sounded as if it was directly over my head. Then, when it seemed to be going away, I ran into Mama's room. She couldn't sleep either. But Sophie and Maria slept right through it all!'

A terrible coldness came over Philip's heart as he listened to her and the facts he had always half suspected and refused to contemplate clicked into place.

'Sophie and Maria are your sisters?' He had to make absolutely certain of what he already guessed to be the truth.

'Yes. They're four years older than me.' She craned her neck to watch the boat being eased into the water.

It was a catastrophe. Worse than the puny drama of the storm. It was the confounding of all his dreams, the pulverising of every minute into a little pile of dust that Emma blew away with every sentence she uttered. But now he had started, he could not stop.

'There are just you and your mother and your sisters here for the summer, then?'

'Oh no, Aunt Jude comes next week,' she replied, her attention still on the boat.

'But at the moment, it's just you and your sisters and . . . '

'Yes.'

There was an enormous splash from the water's edge and a great cheer from the crowd. The boat was afloat once more.

'Did you see!' cried Emma excitedly, turning to Philip. On his face there was a strange look as though the boat had sunk, rather than floated. She wondered what she could do to make amends.

'Were *you* frightened by the thunder last night?' she asked politely, as one might enquire after someone's health.

Philip was in a numb state of silence and shock, as when after a disaster the dust clears and one perceives with incredulity that the sun still shines, and that beneath and beyond the settling rubble the grass is still growing, life continuing. The woman of his dreams was this child's mother. His mouth felt very dry, his head empty. He felt that there would be nothing worth talking about ever again. But out of politeness, he made himself reply. 'I'm afraid I slept through it all – like your sisters.'

'Mama and I couldn't sleep at all, we went and looked out of one of the front bedroom windows to watch the lightning over the sea. It was the most wonderful, terrifying thing! Every time it flashed I jumped, even Mama jumped sometimes. Then suddenly there was the most enormous crash and the sound of glass breaking on the other side of the house. I jumped and Mama shrieked and we rushed out into the passage. We thought lightning had struck the house and it was falling in, or bursting into flames. All the maids woke up and ran downstairs and some of them were crying.'

Emma stared at the distraught look on his face and felt delighted with the effect her recitation was having. 'An old tree near the conservatory had got struck by lightning and fallen into the conservatory and broken all the glass, well, nearly all the glass. But Mr Budge said if it had fallen the other way, it might have fallen against one of the house windows and then we should have had the storm come inside and everything would have been spoiled.'

She drank in the expression of acute concern on his face. She had made Mr Steer's eyes grow very large and pleading. Perhaps he wanted to be told more. 'Mama is in tears,' she added. The eyes in front of her seemed to mist over themselves.

'Miss Emma, don't you go telling fibs!' Dolly's unease at Philip's presence on the quay was increased still further by the effect she saw Emma's words have on him. She tried to take Emma's hand. 'Come on, Miss. Time we was going, we've seen enough disaster for one day.'

'It's not a fib! You weren't there. Mama cried after breakfast when she thought no one could see, and when I hugged her better she said it was the tree. Because it wasn't her house and now the conservatory was all smashed and we'd only just

44

arrived and Papa wasn't here and she didn't know how to get it mended . . . '

'Mr Budge is seeing to all that, you know he is,' said Dolly. She grabbed Emma's hand and tried to pull her away. Emma pushed back.

'Mr Budge is old!' she stormed. She wasn't quite sure afterwards why she had said that, or why it should have had such importance, or why Mr Budge's age rendered him incapable of being any help to her mother. But her outburst prodded Philip out of his lethargy of defeat. One could be, he thought, if not a lover, then a devoted servant.

'If I can help your mother in any way . . . ' Philip blushed.

Emma pulled herself free of Dolly. 'Oh, yes!' She clasped her hands together. 'Let's go at once!' And she turned away from the quayside as though the drama there were finished. 'It's not far,' she added, seeing a slight shadow pass across Mr Steer's face.

It is indeed one thing to indulge in daydreams, in a secret, inner life of dreaming, where one has the power to be more forthright and bold than one is ever capable of in reality. It is even, some would say, one thing to be an idealist, whether one indulges in political idealism or social idealism. But actually to carry out these ideals, even to contemplate drawing the sword out of the sheath of dreams, that is quite another thing, a thing not approved of, especially by a society which had grown great by strict adherence to rules of conduct laid down, as it were, from on high. Anyone, therefore, who went outside these rules, who even threatened them by behaving contrary to expectation, would be regarded as a deviant, a corrupting influence – or a fool. The acceptance that there should be a division between dreaming and reality, even between thoughts expressed over a dinner table and one's actions outside the dining room, comes through exposure to life and the system of rules by which society lives. The gap between things thought, things said and things done is generally held as wisdom, a prudence gained with age. To this, of course, Emma was still immune. When her thoughts were flooded with the possibility of being Mama's saviour, of drying her tears and mending the conservatory by finding a substitute for Papa, who was inconveniently absent, and when Chance had provided the most charming substitute she could have imagined, she had made an instant connection and acted upon it. Her victim's obvious acquiescence to her plans seemed to her only to underline her cleverness. As she trotted along by Mr Steer's side, her head was full of images of Mama hugging her, Mama praising her to Papa, Mama saying, with tears in her eyes, that she didn't know what she would have done without her – and, of course, the delightful image of the discomfort of Sophie and Maria.

The shade that Emma had seen pass across Philip Steer's face was not to be underestimated; it was the stern shade of Victorian morality. Its presence signalled Philip's recognition that, if he acquiesced to Emma's suggestion, he was trespassing in an abhorred region where reality merged into dream. He dimly foresaw the dangers: reality might triumph, and suffocate the dream; or the dream would win, subjecting him to a life that had no basis of fact, no place in the larger life that went on around him. Either way he would be left bereft. But the image of Emma's mother glowed with such intensity that before it the shade of warning was eclipsed.

So he turned, with Emma, away from the quay and strode through the crowd up on to the road that led towards the village. He was aware that his heart beat wildly and that there was a curious shaking in his limbs, while in his head image succeeded image of Emma's mother in various stages of tearfulness and gratefulness, until the images blurred with such passion that by the time they reached the house he was alarmed to find he was unable to construct a clear picture of her at all.

The arrival at the garden gate sobered them all, except for Dolly, who seemed to become more agitated than ever. She had followed them from the quay, tortured by the feeling that she had failed somehow in her duty to her mistress, and, unable to do anything to prevent the disaster she foresaw, was wringing her hands and sobbing 'Oh, lor'!' under her breath. Part of the sobering effect was the simple fact of having arrived at their destination. The house stood there in all its intimidating orderliness, so that by the time they stood at the front door their wild resolve was utterly drained from them. To make matters worse, they could hear men's voices and the sound of sawing coming from somewhere behind the house. The dragon had already been slain.

They stood on the path, disconcerted by the sudden lack of reason for their being there at all. Emma, in a rush of guilt at her over-embellished recitation on the quayside, wanted to burst into tears and run away round the side of the house, and Philip wished fervently that he had never come. Their indecision might have reversed the situation had they remained unseen, had the sound of resolute sawing bitten longer into their consciousness, if one of the maids had not looked out of the dining-room window and seen a remarkably personable young man standing outside on the garden path with Miss Emma, and been immediately and utterly consumed with curiosity to know who he was.

Thus they found themselves suddenly transferred from the garden into a large, dark-panelled hallway. Shafts of sunlight came in from the open drawing-room door and cascaded down a wide staircase to the right, falling in pools of brilliant colour on to the reds and blues of the Turkey carpet. They stood in a hushed cluster by the door.

'Who shall I say, Miss?' whispered the maid, blushing.

'It's Mr Steer,' replied Emma, defiantly. 'He's come to help Mama with the tree.'

The maid turned to him in surprise. 'You came about the tree, sir, as fell down? Well, we got Mr Budge on the tree, sir.'

'No, no,' burst in Emma crossly, 'it's not like that!'

'Oh, lor'!' they heard Dolly moan behind them.

'He's come because Papa is not here.' Emma felt exasperated and frustrated, and suddenly cross with Mr Steer who was causing her all this trouble and with the maids who were being so stupid. She glared up at Mr Steer to try to get him to say something. But he ignored her. He was staring over their heads, and when Emma turned to see what it was he was staring at, she discovered that it was Mama. Mama just standing there in the doorway of the drawing room as though she had been there for a very long time. Mama holding some flowers in her hands whose long, wet stems dripped on to the skirt of her dress, making an ever-widening stain on the pale silk.

The silence that followed seemed to Emma to last an unbearably long time and was punctuated only by the grinding of the saw in the tree, backwards and forwards, increasing the feeling of guilt that grew inside her. Her mother's silence made Mr Steer's presence feel like something wrong, something she ought not to have done. It was a guilt that grew easily; its seed had been there from the moment she had decided to invite Mr Steer home. For she had known, even then, that Mr Budge was looking after the tree for Mama and that there was no possible excuse why she should bring Mr Steer back with her. Now she felt overwhelmed with the fear of having broken the rules. And to compound it, she felt her power over Mr Steer draining away. He was no longer attentive to her, he was ignoring her. Mama was not looking at her either; she was looking at Mr Steer.

It was Nancy who broke the silence. 'This is Mr Steer, ma'am. He's come about the tree . . . ' Her voice trailed away.

Mama glided towards them, and beside her Emma could feel Mr Steer take an urgent step forward to meet her; as their hands touched very briefly, Emma saw how suddenly large Mr Steer's tapering fingers seemed next to Mama's. How the ends of their fingers scarcely touched and then parted. Like two fish she had seen once in an aquarium who drifted together on a current of water and, shocked by the gentle impact of their bodies, darted apart again.

'I must apologise for disturbing your household on a morning which I understand is already full of catastrophe. Emma and I met the other day, and this morning on the quay she told me of your distress over the tree – and the conservatory. I thought, or rather Emma thought – that is to say I hoped, that I could be of some assistance to you.'

Mama's confusion seemed as great as his. She twisted the flowers between her fingers and smiled shyly at him. 'It was kind of you to call. I'm very grateful.'

The sawing continued, mercilessly grinding into the fallen tree. Philip gestured towards the sound. 'You seem, in fact, to have no lack of willing helpers.'

'The gardener, and some men from the village. They have dragged the tree clear of the glass and are sawing it up.' Mama's voice was not her usual one, and she paused between phrases as though not quite sure what to say next, as if she were unwilling to speak at all. 'But please, do give Nancy your coat and come into the drawing room.'

Mr Steer's coat was taken, and then his cap, and then he seemed to be bending down to take off his shoes.

'My galoshes,' he explained, tugging at the overshoes and going red in the face.

'You fear another storm, Mr Steer?'

'I hate getting my feet wet.'

After the darkness of the hall, the drawing room seemed full of light. Mama led the way with Mr Steer beside her. Emma followed a little distance behind. They had both withdrawn from her into their adult world, moving together across the room, turning their heads to each other as they spoke in voices too inaudible for Emma to catch what they were saying. They reached the windows overlooking the garden and the conservatory and stood together watching the men repairing the damage as though it were a play put on for their benefit.

It was not quite the hero's welcome Emma had envisaged earlier in the morning, this exclusion. She had not seen herself skulking at the back of the drawing room. She had not taken into account the possibility of Mr Steer's defection any more than she had imagined that Mama would ignore her presence in such a disturbing way. She wanted very much to join them at the window, to enlarge upon the disaster of the tree, to have them listen to her and to feel the same magic power she had felt briefly at the quayside. But if Mama was cross with her then she might send her to her room for interrupting and then her disgrace in front of Mr Steer would be complete. So she stayed where she was, running her finger up and down the polished beading on the top of the grand piano, until Mama half-turning from the window caught sight of her, was almost startled by seeing her, as though she had forgotten she was there.

'Emma, ask Nancy to bring us some hot chocolate. Will you have some hot chocolate with us, Mr Steer?'

He said nothing, but smiled first at Mama and then at Emma, who felt her friendship restored and skipped towards the fireplace where the bell-cord hung. Usually they argued fiercely, Emma, Maria and Sophie, about whose turn it was to summon one of the maids, for it was not something they were allowed to do without permission. Now Emma could glory in that grandness alone.

'No, Emma!' Her mother's voice was sharp. 'Go and ask Nancy in the kitchen.'

'Can't I pull the sash?'

'No.' Her mother turned back to the window.

By the time Emma returned, her mother was seated on one sofa and Mr Steer faced her on the other. The room felt very calm and warm. Emma went and stood between them. 'I did it,' she announced.

They broke off from their conversation.

'What?' asked her mother.

'Told Nancy.'

They did not immediately begin talking again. Emma felt a vague, malicious pleasure at having disturbed them and began to walk slowly up and down the squares on the Indian rug before the fireplace, walking on the tips of her toes with great care and deliberation. Hesitantly, the conversation began again and Emma guessed that they were talking about London. She listened absent-mindedly, giving most of her attention to not stepping out of the squares. Mama was discovering that Mr Steer was a painter. *She* knew that already. Then they began to recite names of places that they both knew, with smiles of delight, as though they were swapping marbles. Emma lost interest in them and instead turned the carpet into a chase of life and death, where danger lurked in every lozenge and hid in every rose, and those who stumbled off the path of squares were instantly lost. She tiptoed faster and faster, until the ground beneath her feet became a dizzying swirl of reds and blues and gold. The sun came out from behind tattered clouds and the colours beneath her feet shone like inlaid jewels. She heard her mother laugh once; the sound broke into her bedazzled brain like a sound outside a dream, and she nearly lost her footing. She went faster and faster, her body swaying above feet that were beginning to lose their sureness in the momentum that carried them on. They landed dangerously lopsided in the squares, almost overbalancing into disaster. Once or twice she nearly tripped and when at last, completely dizzy, one foot landed wide of the mark, she shrieked in terror.

'Emma!'

She felt her arm grabbed and jumped with fright.

'Emma!'

She looked round. Everything seemed to swim with the colours of the carpet, and as they subsided she became aware of a world outside her own, watching her. Mama was leaning forward to steady her, Mr Steer was smiling his soft smile and Nancy was standing on the edge of the hearthrug with a silver tray in her hands.

'Emma, come and sit out of Nancy's way.'

Emma wobbled on to a footstool at her mother's side and leaned against her knee, feeling the room spin round, watching Nancy pour out the chocolate with an almost drunken intensity. Nancy looked preoccupied and slightly troubled, and when she brought Emma's chocolate she did not smile, but said in a low voice, 'Take care, Miss Emma, to hold it straight,' leaving directly to hear more of Dolly Brown's stories about the goings-on of Mr Philip Steer.

In the drawing room the adults sipped their chocolate in silence as though suddenly constrained by having Emma's undivided attention. Emma, surprised by the silence, into which the delicate chinking of cups against saucers sounded unnaturally loud, looked from one bent head to another and wondered if she shouldn't re-open the conversation by describing to her mother the events on the quay.

But just then Mr Steer spoke. 'What made you choose Walberswick for a holiday?'

'In a way my aunt chose it for us,' replied Isobel. 'She lives now in Southwold and, knowing that Colonel and Mrs James, who are out in India, would let their house to certain families, wrote to them on our behalf. The fact that my aunt was also free to spend the summer with us made the prospect irresistible.' Isobel smiled across at Philip. 'But what brings you here?'

'I come here to paint. I've been coming here every summer for several years. A lot of painters come here, or used to come here; it was a painter friend of mine who had a studio in the same house in Chelsea as I did, who first brought me. I'd just come back from studying in Paris and that first summer in Manresa Road I couldn't settle to anything. He got so sick of my moping that he dragged me down here with him one weekend at the beginning of August. We hired horses and rode all over the parish and beyond. I remember we even took them across the chain ferry to Southwold. I fell in love with the place there and then and I come back every summer. There's something about the light here, the way it reflects off the sea . . . ' His voice trailed away as if he were suddenly lost in his own thoughts.

'Mama!' Emma jumped up.

'Shhhh.' Her mother too seemed lost in Mr Steer's words.

'Mama! Mayn't we have horses and go exploring too and have picnics in the woods, the way you used to with your brothers and sisters?'

'I don't think there are any woods round here, my sweet,' replied her mother.

'Oh, there are!' exclaimed Philip. 'There are several coverts dotted about on high ground above the marsh. But the best is a proper wood,' he smiled down at Emma, 'called Foxburrow Wood, on the road to Dunwich. It has rides and vistas and the most charming spots for picnicking.' He paused. 'I should be delighted to show it to you.'

'Oh yes, Mama, do say yes.'

'I'm quite sure we could hire a chaise,' ventured Philip.

'I understand,' began Isobel slowly, as if not quite convinced of the wisdom or propriety of imparting her information, 'that the Colonel's chaise is kept for him by someone in the village and that it is at our disposal while we are here.'

'Then we can have all kinds of excursions,' exclaimed Emma, jumping up.

'We'll see, Emma, when Aunt Jude comes.'

Philip stood up; he straightened the sleeves of his jacket with a precise, almost military manner and did up one button of his coat as if to indicate that the conversation was closed. 'I must go,' he said.

Isobel rose swiftly, as though to prevent him leaving. But instead, she rang the bell for Nancy. Emma, perplexed at the sudden disruption, watched Mama and Mr Steer walk together out of the circle of sofas towards the French windows, as though moving out of earshot of an assembled company. She felt forbidden to follow. Mr Steer spoke to Mama in a low voice that Emma could hardly hear. 'I should be honoured if you would allow me to show you and your family a little of the surrounding countryside.'

Mama was silent, looking out over the lawn. Mr Steer was watching Mama's face intently. He seemed not at all interested in the garden. 'Will your aunt join you soon?' he began again, in the same low, urgent voice.

Nancy entered the drawing room and hesitated at the door, but neither of them noticed her.

'In about a week,' replied Mama softly, still gazing straight ahead.

'May I call again, then?'

Emma saw Mama turn her head at last and smile. 'Yes.' And all the anxiety in Mr Steer's face smoothed out. They both turned out of their privacy back into the room.

'Nancy,' said Mama briskly, 'Mr Steer is leaving.'

Chapter Five

When Sophie and Maria discovered they had missed Mr Steer's visit they were beside themselves with rage. They refused to speak to Emma for a whole day. So Emma floated, after all, on a brief cloud of glory, elated by the sullen silence of her sisters. For the next few days the little girls hardly left their mother's side for fear of missing some other handsome stranger. They practised their curtsies and fussed over the tying of each other's sashes, and were rewarded for their dutifulness by a constant stream of old ladies as the rest of the village followed Philip's visit with curiosity calls of their own.

The leader in matters social was the vicar's wife, who had the added distinction of being able to call herself a neighbour.

'My dear!' she exclaimed on being ushered into Isobel's drawing room; and, sailing immediately to the door which led to the conservatory, 'Why, your disaster is quite mended!'

There was a look, as Sophie confided later to Maria, almost of disappointment on her face. She turned her back on the conservatory and surveyed the little family.

'Ah,' she said, for want of anything pleasant, and gave them a strange, strangled smile that was almost a grimace. Her eyes moved from face to face. She found Isobel disagreeably pretty in a wan sort of way, hardly looking old enough to have borne such grown-up children. Too grown-up, especially the elder girls, and too handsome for their own good; bold eyes they had, especially the darker one; from their father no doubt. And where was he? As for that little one, grinning from ear to ear, standing in front of all the others, instead of modestly in the background with downcast eyes. Mrs Rount took a step forward. Such unseemly eagerness should be rectified. She opened her arms as she bore down on Emma, with a fierce glitter in her eyes and a grim smile twisting her mouth, ready to crush her to her bosom. But Emma was determined to vanquish the whole village with her welcomes. She emerged from Mrs Rount's embrace gasping for breath, her cheek stinging from the spiky crystals of a brooch, with a fixed smile on her face, and answered Mrs Rount's interrogation with such an unswerving belief in her social success that she was, at least, not defeated.

The Misses Mayhew plucked up courage to call on Isobel, mainly through fear of Mrs Rount's sharp tongue if they did not, but also to quiet the insatiable twittering of their curiosity. They arrived the following morning in lavender-coloured hats and lace gloves and expressed themselves delighted with everything they saw. Isobel enchanted them, the little girls enchanted them, the way the flowers were arranged in the drawing room enchanted them. But as soon as they were back home they could talk of nothing but their disappointment at not meeting *Mr* Heatherington.

Soon Maria and Sophie gave up hope of there being another fairy prince in so poor a village and even Emma's smiles paled. They decided, instead, to spend every afternoon on the beach. This particular afternoon they were all paddling at the edge of the sea with their skirts hitched up so as not to get wet. The pleasure of having bare legs and poking around in the shallows together for shells, seaweed, starfish and pearls softened the feelings of the two elder sisters towards Emma, who was, it must be admitted, being remarkably helpful and more quick-eyed than they about finding things. Besides, she had information that as yet they had been too proud to ask her to divulge. They had plagued Nancy for details of Philip's appearance, but she couldn't tell them what he had said to Mama and what she had said to him. And besides, a maid's opinion was not quite the same.

'Emma,' drawled Sophie.

'Mmm.'

'Emma, when you said the other day you'd already met Mr Steer, what did you mean "met"?'

'I did, I met him,' said Emma, gazing into the water, where a piece of seaweed floated on the current; up and down, up . . .

'Well, who introduced you? You can't just *meet* people.'

'Dolly did.'

'Dolly did!' Sophie stared at her little sister with horror. Behind Emma's back, Maria shook her head slowly at her sister.

Sophie's eyes narrowed. 'You're lying. How could one of the maids introduce you.'

Emma turned from the undulating seaweed, put her hands on her hips and faced Sophie belligerently. 'She did so!'

Sophie raised her eyebrows.

'What did she do so?' mimicked Maria.

Emma stamped in the water and her sisters darted out of the way. 'We met him in a field and Dolly knew him because he used to paint her picture and he said he'd paint me!' she shouted at them. They advanced on her, kicking the water and covering her with spray. Emma kicked back until they were all soaked – and then, as suddenly as the water fight had begun, it ended. She turned away from her sisters and began to walk along the edge of the foam, scuffling in the spray with her toes.

'Baby, baby,' her sisters called after her, and waited for her to come back so that they could continue their cross-questioning. They sat down at the edge of the water, where the sand was just dry and yet they could have their feet in the sea.

'She is a plague,' murmured Sophie to Maria as they watched her wander further and further along the shore. They were surprised to see her strike suddenly inland over the beach towards the dunes. And then they noticed a solitary figure sitting hunched up on the sand.

He didn't move at all, even when Emma got right up close to him. It was only when a shadow fell across the white paper on his knee that he suddenly looked up.

'Hello,' said Emma.

'Ah . . .' He looked up at her vaguely, with eyes that seemed so wide open it was as if they were trying to catch expression out of the air, rather than give it. 'Nearly through,' he said, and turned back to his drawing.

Emma sat down beside him in the sand and watched. The paper was covered not only with lines, but with words, in writing too grown-up for Emma to be able to read. There were squiggly lines for waves and bits of writing even between the waves. Then there was a large white space for beach and within that space a cluster of short, jagged lines, scarcely joined up at all when you looked close. A woman sat bolt upright with a parasol and just two smudge-lines for her face, from which you knew immediately that it was fat and pink and hot and that she would have little pig-eyes that stared straight out to sea without seeing it at all, dazzled by the sun on the water, longing to be somewhere else. A girl lay on her back with two matchstick arms crossed over her face to keep the sun off in such a way that Emma could feel over her own face the hot stifle of muslin sleeves, and hear in her own ears the droning and splinter-shrieks of the afternoon beach.

Philip's pencil darted at the paper, striking it and leaving black marks at every stroke. The pencil was as magic as the apparently random marks it made with such fevered urgency. It seemed to be digging the lines up out of the paper as though it knew they lay hidden there, buried alive. Philip began to write more words on the drawing, in the blank spaces of paper between each person, and sometimes the words went on over the person.

'Why are you writing on it?' asked Emma.

'It's to remind me,' replied Philip without looking up. 'If I decide to turn this sketch into a painting, I need to remember what colour everything is. I might forget the pink of that girl's skirt – the way it goes pinky-blue in the folds where she's lying on it and almost white on top where the sunshine bleaches out the colour. It's beautiful, but I might forget it, so I leave myself clues. Then, whenever I look at this sketch again, I shall see this beach and this afternoon, just as it was.'

'I wish I could draw like that. Are there any more?'

Philip turned back a page to show the sheet below. It was covered with parasols – hands holding parasols, parasols from above with shoulders below and foreshortened backs sticking strangely out, side views and front views of faces beneath parasols. Philip turned another page.

'Oh,' exclaimed Emma, 'it's us!'

He'd sketched them like three storks at the water's edge, ripples in wavy lines lapping at their long, stick-like legs, their dresses tucked up into their sashes like folded feathers, heads bent, peering into the water, as though for fish. Two of them were holding hands with their backs to the beach, while the third faced the shore, one arm delving into the water.

'That's me,' said Emma almost to herself, touching the bent figure wonderingly with her finger and seeing, as clearly as if she were looking at it through translucent water once again, the undulating strand of seaweed. It lived for a moment longer, turning and sinuating languorously in the current, and then, as she moved her finger, it faded.

'Will you make a painting of us?'

'I might.'

'Will you?' breathed Emma.

Philip smiled into her flushed face. She seemed suddenly aware of an importance and a beauty that she had never hitherto felt for herself. The infinite delusion of vanity with all its miasma of delight opened up before her, and he saw in her eyes how she let herself be carried away by it.

'What colour will my dress be?' she asked dreamily.

'Why, the colour that it is.'

'Oh!'

Philip tried hard not to laugh at the surprise and disappointment on her face. To be the subject of a painting was almost a fantasy; people thought that only things expressing beauty or perfection were painted, that being in a painting at all meant that one was beautiful, or if not beautiful, then made beautiful. Emma did not expect to be painted in her pink and white striped cotton dress, just as it was, tucked unceremoniously into her sash.

'I spend all my time trying to paint things as they really are,' said Philip. 'Not just pretty things, everything. Look at the sea.' He pointed out over the beach. 'I don't just want to paint it blue. I want to paint its wetness, its restlessness, the way the sun sparkles on it and the waves bounce back the light into the air and how almost every wave is a different colour. I want to paint sunshine so that you feel its heat when you look at it, so that the paint is a dense shimmer that dazzles you.'

Emma turned her head from contemplation of the sea and looked solemnly at him. 'I just paint it yellow,' she said, 'when I paint the sun. That's the colour it is.'

They sat in a hollow in the sand-dunes. Emma burrowed her feet in the warm sand and let it trickle through her toes. Philip watched her with a kind of plaintive enviousness in his eyes. She had such utter simplicity in her approach to life. He looked at the way her bare toes wriggled with pleasure in the sand and how his own were encased, shut away from such feelings, in heavy boots.

She came again to find him the next day, sidling off from her sisters and climbing up the sand-dunes in a flurry of loose sand. She thought he would be annoyed at her interruption, but she was surprised to feel how pleased he was. He knew she would come; he knew that she was drawn by a craving to see again her own image. For all her childishness, she reminded him of the young models who sat for him in Chelsea. They did it not just for the money he paid them, but for their glorification in paint.

'You look hot,' said Philip.

Emma grinned at him. Freckles were beginning to appear on her cheeks and her legs were losing their London pallor.

'We've been playing tag. Did you see us?'

Her hair hung in tendrils round her face and she reached up to push them back from her cheeks.

'Why don't you sit over there on that hump of sand, and I'll draw you.'

'Here?' She darted over to another tussock of grass. 'Or here?'

Philip stretched out his legs and turned over the page in his sketchbook. He began to sketch rapidly, pausing every few seconds to look up at Emma, who stared proudly back at him from her tuft of grass. She thought how strange the expression on Philip's face had gone; it had become laced up with a taut urgency, and his eyes had got smaller and fiercer so that they seemed to look right inside her without noticing her face at all. She wondered what he was drawing.

'Can I take it home and show Mama?'

'No,' said Philip, 'not this one. I have a rule that I don't ever tear pages out of these notebooks.'

'Oh,' replied Emma, downcast. Sophie and Maria would never believe her.

They sat in silence on the sand-dune. From time to time a little wind ruffled the pages of the sketchbook and blew Emma's hair across her face. Sometimes a gull floated over their heads, balancing itself, tipping its body to ride in the air currents across the beach and then low over the waves, hunting lazily through the afternoon.

'Mama is coming down to the beach for tea.'

'Is she?'

'Yes. Mrs Freestone said she would make a sandcake for Mama to bring.' Emma giggled. 'Imagine, a *sandcake*! Ugh!'

As Emma's giggles subsided she remembered her concern to show her sisters the drawing. 'I'm sure Mama would let you come to tea. She won't be long.' Something, it struck her, had changed in Philip's face. 'You would like to see her again, wouldn't you?'

For the past three days Philip had thought of nothing else but when he could see Isobel again. He had gone over their meeting word by word, look by look, the image of Isobel's face sliding in and out of all his thoughts, their words becoming confused by repetition until he could not tell where memory ended and dream began. The temptation to see her again was great.

'When does your aunt arrive?'

The significance of the question was lost on Emma, who was merely puzzled by the non-sequitur and the haunted expression on Philip's face.

'On Friday – but won't you stay and have tea with us, so everyone can see my picture?' she wheedled.

'No,' said Philip hastily. 'No.' He began to pack his things away jerkily, like a marionette whose strings were pulled by an unsympathetic master. 'I have to go and see someone. I promised.'

After the echoing noise of the beach, Mr Smytheson's garden, muffled by its immense trees and bushes, was warm and silent. Philip found the old man sitting stiffly on one of the straight-backed dining chairs on the terrace at the back of the house, a straw boater perched on his head and a plaid travelling rug over his shoulders. He slowly swivelled his whole body round as he heard Philip approach.

'Ah, dear boy,' he cried and carefully swivelled back to his former position, motioning Philip to a chair in front of him. 'Bit stiff still, you know.'

'It's good to see you up and about.' Philip sank into the low canvas chair and smiled up at the old man.

'Been paintin'?'

'Yes, I've been out on the dunes, drawing people on the beach. Models for free, you might say.'

'How goes it?'

'Oh,' Philip sighed, and shrugged, as though the question were more about love than art. 'How are you?' he added, to change the subject.

The old man beamed. 'Bandages off in five days!' He tapped his stick on the ground for emphasis. 'Five days and I'll be hoppin' around like the Misses Mayhew. They came to visit me this mornin',' he chuckled, 'twitterin' about having met your Mrs Heatherington. Quite put out they were when I said you'd met her first.'

'My Mrs Heatherington,' thought Philip miserably. 'Mine! How can she ever be mine?'

Tea came and was set between them on little tables that wobbled on the uneven flagstones of the terrace. The afternoon drowsed on, and stealthily the shadows of the great yew trees advanced across the grass.

By the time Philip left it was early evening. He did not go immediately back to the inn but made his way towards the estuary, walking across the common behind Smytheson's house. Below him a boat slipped slowly up river on the evening tide, bumped softly into her mooring berth and was tied up for the night. Farther on a girl passed him, leading a goat up from the marshes. Everything around him had an order of its own into which it was gently subsiding. Eventually his path came in view of the back of Quay House. The high wall hid the garden and lower rooms from view; only the upper storey was visible. Philip stared into the blank glass of the bedroom windows and the hopelessness of his passion seemed to stare back. It was futile, pointless; and if it were not – it would be worse. It would shatter the order of both their lives and they would be condemned to live in disorder, the whole crushing weight of society's disapproval for ever on their backs. In so short a time the warm luxury of possessiveness that he had experienced in Smytheson's garden had given way to the numbing cold of renunciation. The men on the quayside were going through their usual evening rituals with devotional slowness. A group stood talking near the ferry; two boys threw pebbles at a seagull perched out of reach on a channel marker; and an old man squelched past Philip cradling an anchor in his arms as though it were a baby. From the far side of the estuary, a man rowed towards them in a little coracle; the oars dipped into the water and rose again in a slow arc. Another fisherman sat on the steps of one of the stilted huts and folded yard after yard of fishing-net into a neat stack with such nonchalance it seemed to flow through his fingers like water. But Philip had no heart for such calm: it jarred on him in a cacophony and he walked on. Between the huts to the right, a wooden bridge crossed the Dunwich river just before it flowed into the sea, and there Philip stood, leaning on the low rails for a moment. To his right lay the deserted beach and ahead of him stretched an infinity of water over which a lone gull flew, making for the harbour. Philip turned his head slowly to keep the gull in sight, marvelling at its ability to ride the currents of air; it lifted suddenly over the pier which marked the entrance to the estuary, and Philip's heart missed a beat. At the very end of the pier, standing motionless, staring out to sea, was Isobel. Around her ran Emma and her sisters, chasing each other, shrieking with delight. But Isobel stood, as though utterly alone, gripping the top rail, her body leaning forward as though unwillingly confined behind the bars, staring out at the horizon.

Chapter Six

Aunt Jude was a woman who shone with enthusiasm for life. It was held in tight with numerous small buttons, tied in swathes with broad sashes; it was jacketed, shawled and enveloped in capes – but it threatened always to escape. It bubbled out into beads of jet, jingling fringes and splatters of sequins, stuck here and there with sparkling brooches and hung about with necklaces. She seemed to be at once unwillingly confining it for the sake of decorum and unashamedly celebrating it. Her voice was soft and continuous like honey trickling from a jar, as compelling as a blackbird singing in the silence that follows rain. Often, when she was not speaking, she would accompany the conversation with a companionable breathing sound, as though her gregarious nature could not bear to remain silent. In fact, Aunt Jude was asthmatic. Emma was enthralled by the prolonged wheeze that sometimes escaped her aunt, as though there were a pair of bellows lodged deep inside her chest. She was fond of hugging people, and Emma, basking in such affectionate attention with her ear crushed against her aunt's bosom, would listen, fascinated, to the repertoire of hissings and whisperings. Aunt Jude tried to bestow her affection also on Maria and Sophie, but with less success. They were growing into perfect Victorians and disliked such noisy expressions of affection. Moreover, she was, they declared, a provincial.

It was this very link with her country childhood that was so precious to Isobel. She was relieved to find that her aunt had changed scarcely at all from the Aunt Jude of her youth, who was so overwhelmingly efficient at life, who could draw pleasure from the smallest thing and express it and expand it and share it out among whomever was present until the thing itself, held in everyone's attention, grew in importance. And when Aunt Jude gathered in the pieces again from each of them, the smallest thing was seen to have been transformed into something gigantic. It was this magician's touch that had captivated Isobel as a child. She had followed her aunt like a little, silent devotee all through those long summers filled with the ebb and flow of guests and relations who flooded the house and the parkland and left it again, warm and dry and echoing. She watched Aunt Jude perform her magic day after day with a kind of yearning for the same facility to dissolve all the difficulties with which she struggled. And when, at the end of the summer, Aunt Jude left, Isobel had tentatively stretched out her own hand to transform life, and found it disappointingly cold to the touch.

Aunt Jude's reappearance enabled Isobel to slide back into a time when she had no responsibility, when she could be an insignificant member of a large household, instead of its head. Aunt Jude came as a guest to Quay House, and from the subtle position of second in command she came to be its driving force. The house under Isobel had merely functioned; with the arrival of Aunt Jude, it began softly to hum.

Isobel sat one morning in the drawing room trying to compose a list of preparations for the picnic they were to have the next day. Aunt Jude had announced a wish to explore the village and had departed with Emma, Maria, Sophie and an armoury of walking-sticks and umbrellas. Isobel had no inspiration for making lists that morning. She sat in the tremulous sunshine that wavered, grew strong and faded again as rain-clouds drifted across the garden. She thought of what she should wear for the outing; of where they should go; of the moment when Mr Steer might offer his arm to her. Gazing at the room around her, she pondered on how suddenly it had lost its strangeness and become familiar, how it now formed a back-drop for their lives instead of being a still-life into which she intruded. In the comforting presence of Aunt Jude, she felt as though a weight had been lifted from her. A vague sense of fear, of something in the house sliding beyond her control, had disappeared.

Philip felt it too. He had approached the house for his second visit with even more trepidation than he had for the first, and to his surprise he found the atmosphere quite changed. He was struck by a certain boldness and openness, even in the way Nancy opened the door to him and announced his presence to the assembled drawing room. They were all gathered there:

Isobel, Emma, the two elder sisters, whom he had not yet met, and Aunt Jude. He had expected Aunt Jude to be formidable and tight-lipped and to regard him with suspicion. Instead, she gleamed with welcome, quivering watered silk like a raindrop reflecting sunshine. There was a warm clicking of beads around her neck and a glitter of rings on her fingers as he bowed quickly over them; then a breathless stream of questions, uttered in a low voice, which he did not at first identify as being asthmatic, but as embarrassingly intimate. He became so overcome with confusion that he could barely answer one question before she broke in with the next. And the more his confusion grew, the more tenderly she smiled at him.

His catechism over, the conversation became more general, and he was then subjected to intense scrutiny by Emma's elder sisters. Finally, he was able to voice his proposal that he be permitted to show the family a few of the beauty spots in the surrounding countryside, suggesting that they might all drive to picnic in Foxburrow Wood.

In the immediate uproar of delight that exploded around her, Isobel was amused to see how everyone turned to her for approbation. It seemed like a scene from a play where everyone was pretending to be one thing, knowing full well that in reality they were quite another. They were pretending that she might refuse Mr Steer's invitation, when surely they must know refusal was the last thing in her mind, and that Mr Steer was inviting all five of them because that was the only way he could be with just one of them for a whole afternoon. She felt sure they must be able to see that, just from looking at Mr Steer's face. But they weren't looking in his direction at all; they were looking at her.

'Mama, do say yes,' begged Maria.

'Isobel my dear,' said Aunt Jude, 'what do you think? It's an enchanting place in early summer. The children would adore it.'

Emma jumped from square to square of the carpet, ending up in front of her mother, and twined her arms round her neck. 'Mama,' she whispered in her ear, 'say we can go!'

Isobel laughed. Over the top of Emma's head she could see directly into the anxiety in Mr Steer's eyes. All else was propriety and even reticence. He was quiet in a way that was not at all 'artistic' – just as his country suits were surprisingly well made and his drawing-room manners were perfect. It was precisely this unexpectedness that arrested one's attention, and then, one's attention drawn, something else in him held it very gently . . .

'Of course,' she said, watching the lines on his face soften, with a growing feeling of uncurling power, 'a drive would be perfect.'

So it was settled that if Thursday were fair, they would take a picnic to Foxburrow Wood.

In the event the weather was fair. That was to say it did not rain. It was like so many days in an English summer, uniformly grey, a pale grey with neither a break in the smooth, high cloud, nor an ominous massing of it. The colonel's dogcart was kept, in his absence, at Eastwoodlodge Farm. On Thursday, soon after lunch, it was sent down, with one of the ploughmen in his Sunday best as driver, to collect the party from Quay House, and Philip joined them as they stopped at 'The Anchor' on their way out of the village. He found himself squeezed in at the end of the cart, next to Sophie and opposite Aunt Jude, about as far from Isobel's side as it was possible to be. Emma must have seen a slight disappointment cross his face for she leaned forward and assured him that the picnic baskets were safely stowed in the front under the driver's seat. They trotted past the long nave of the church, leaving the village behind, and the heath, broken by clumps of pine trees, opened up around them. It was all heather and bracken and stretches of gorse-bush covered in bright yellow flowers. Birds flew up from hidden nests at the sound of the wheels and a kestrel hung motionless in the pale air. They slowed only once, to cross the railway line that ran from Southwold across Walberswick Common to Halesworth, and then raced on. The road twisted and turned. It was bounded by hedges for a short stretch, and then emerged beside an open field that ran down to Blythburgh Mere, which shone grey, like silver; hatched with small waves, the pale, polished sky rising in an arc over it. It was like driving along the rim of a silver bowl. The pony picked up his heels and they all clutched at their hats, the exhilaration of the sudden speed making their delight soar. Their eyes shone, their mouths opened involuntarily; they gazed around them at the spreading panorama and at each other as though everything had taken on a new wonder.

'Oh, Mama!' breathed Emma, twisting in her seat to see the shining water.

'Yes,' whispered Isobel. Her heart contracted so tight she had to gasp for breath. She was overwhelmed by the nearness of Mr Steer, the speed at which her thoughts raced and the wind that whirled inside her.

Philip could not bring himself to look at Isobel. To see her look back at him would force him to try to explain all that he felt, all that he saw – the colour and the light and the movement. And if he tried, he would wave his hands ineffectually and the wind would tear away his words before she had caught them. Worst of all, she might not understand. It was safer to smile at Aunt Jude when the moment of exhilaration had passed, to point out to her the various landmarks; the approaching tower of Blythburgh Church and the distant town of Southwold huddled by the sea.

They turned left at the crossroads before Blythburgh, and then again a mile further on, as though doubling back on their tracks in a parallel line. Now the heath gave way to a neat plantation of young pines. The trees were low and spaced, running away on either side of the road into long rides, wedges of forest full of a delicate green light, so that they felt they were in the depths of another country. The pony slowed to a walk. The afternoon seemed trapped in the quiet of the leafy road, with its neat grass verges and snatches of birdsong, and the wildness of the heath was forgotten.

'Mama!' exclaimed Maria. 'It's so pretty!'

'This is Foxburrow Wood,' announced Philip.

It was decided to let Emma choose which ride they should picnic in, a responsibility that immediately overwhelmed her. As the pony ambled on, the rides flickered past, tunnels opening at their far end to a jewel-like brightness of sunlight at the other side of the wood. They were like ivory spokes in a jade fan. Light, dark, light, dark – Emma was mesmerised. She looked and looked and felt she could not see.

'Here! Here!' cried her sisters every time an opening appeared in the trees. 'This one!'

'Leave her alone,' laughed Aunt Jude, 'let her choose.'

Philip began to feel concerned that they would soon be out of the wood. To have to turn round and come back looking for a place to picnic would somehow mar the perfection of the outing. Isobel saw the glazed anxiety in Emma's face. She caught sight of a break in the trees a few yards ahead, bent down, and whispered in her ear, 'Now.'

'Now!' shouted Emma, and was as alarmed as everyone else by the loudness of her own voice.

The pony was halted and they all climbed out of the dogcart with admonitions to each other to take care. The solid ground felt strange beneath their feet after the swaying motion, and they stood together in a somewhat uncertain group. The driver led the horse and cart away to a respectable distance and began to uncouple the heavy harness.

'Well!' said Philip, as jovially as he could. There was in the air a feeling that it had been more fun travelling than arriving.

Aunt Jude bent down and picked up the smaller of the two baskets. 'I think perhaps some tea, Isobel, after all that excitement.'

'Some tea would be very welcome, Aunt. Come girls, let's spread the rugs out. Sophie and Maria, take that brown one . . .'

Tea was unpacked in a glitter of silver hot-water flasks and lidded cream and sugar jugs, delicate little sandwiches were piled on china as fine as that at home in Lowndes Square. A large, glistening plum-cake took pride of place, surrounded by plates of tiny scones, and silver pots of jam, and thick cream to spread inside them.

Philip could eat nothing. He took a sandwich from the first plate that was offered to him, but although he picked it up several times as though to bite it, each time he put it down again. He drank several cups of tea, hoping to clear his throat of the absurd obstruction that prevented him from saying anything more than a monosyllable here and there. Aunt Jude and the children, however, kept up an animated conversation about gypsies.

Isobel ate one minute sandwich after another. She knew that if she kept filling her mouth with food, Philip would be too polite to ask her a question until he could see it was empty. But Philip, as soon as he saw her finish one sandwich, offered her another in the hope that action would prompt him into speech.

Words still failed him, so their exchange was limited to shy glances across diminishing plates of tiny sandwiches.

When tea was over the party broke up. Sophie and Maria went to feed the remaining sandwiches to the horse that stood with its eyes closed. As they approached, it lifted an eyelid and gazed at them through long lashes. It ate the sandwiches with no special show of delight or gratitude and closed its eyes again. Maria and Sophie skirted with some distaste the outstretched body of the driver, who slept noisily with his mouth half open and his shirt unbuttoned. Emma knelt in front of her mother, staring over Isobel's shoulder up the ride of green turf to the distant triangle at the end of the wood which shone like brightly coloured glass: blue and green and gold. The hot, summery world beyond the forest.

She put her arms round her mother's neck. 'Come with me for a walk up the path through the forest to where it's all bright and sunny.'

'It's bright and sunny here,' smiled Isobel.

'Come with me a little way.'

'Ask Maria and Sophie, I think they're already in the wood.'

'They won't come.' Emma got up and wandered off.

Philip and Isobel sat amid the ruins of the picnic with Aunt Jude, sitting all three in silence, staring in different directions, absorbed by the warmth and the quiet and a sense of waiting. Isobel felt suddenly hot under her shawl and unclasped it. Philip saw how very soft the curve of her neck was. He looked away and caught Aunt Jude watching him, her eyes glittering as though she comprehended his desire. Philip, embarrassed, waved an arm in the air to indicate the scene before him, and a blackbird flew away shrieking.

'It's so beautiful,' he said, to redirect her attention.

Aunt Jude smiled and remembered all the perfect summers she had seen.

Isobel looked up at him. 'Doesn't it make you want to paint it?'

Philip gazed back at her. 'Will you allow me to paint you?' he blurted out.

Isobel blushed. 'I meant the wood.'

'Let Mr Steer draw you *and* the trees, Isobel dear,' interposed Aunt Jude. 'What a picture she would make, wouldn't she, Mr

Steer!' She became all arrangement and fluster. 'Tilt your head back a little, dear, so we can see your face. There,' she beamed, 'that's right,' and nodded knowingly at the apparent innocence of Isobel's confusion.

Obediently, Isobel rearranged her hat and smoothed out her skirts. Philip drew his painting-box towards him and took out his sketch-book. Their preparations complete, they looked up at each other across the silence, too shy to begin. Aunt Jude remained discreetly still. Isobel cleared her throat. 'How . . . how shall I sit?'

'Oh,' said Philip breathlessly, 'just as you are, please, don't move anything. I mean – do move; don't sit still for my sake. I like the person I'm drawing to be natural and animated. To sit too still often makes the drawing lifeless.'

Philip tried the first few tentative strokes. Aunt Jude sat, as though at an entertainment, eagerly watching them both. Philip felt quite unable to continue.

'Would you, er, talk to Mrs Heatherington?'

'Of course, of course!' Aunt Jude bent towards her niece, wheezing importantly. 'Did I tell you, Isobel, of my visit to Henrietta and her little boys last month?'

The more Philip stared at Isobel, the more immobilised he found himself. The metamorphosis from body into shape that his sitters usually underwent within a few moments of his picking up his pencil refused to take place. Isobel did not slide from identity into objectivity; it was as though Philip had no power any more to throw the switch that would set the transformation in motion. She remained – Isobel. It was her brow and nose and mouth and chin that he tried to outline on paper, and as he did so he felt he was stroking them with his finger. He not so much saw their outline as felt it, as though the paper, where his pencil touched it, were transformed into skin and flesh. From time to time he saw her eyes wander from her aunt's face to his, as though she knew how he stared, and she would smile at him apologetically. Behind them in the wood the three girls darted like moths in their pale dresses.

'Mama!' called Emma, 'we've found some bluebells.'

But no one answered her. The grown-ups sat on the rugs, bent towards each other, totally absorbed in each other, and Mama did not even turn her head.

The drive home was quiet and slow as though evening had overtaken them all. The light had not faded, nor the sky changed, but there was a drawn-out feeling to the day. Foxburrow Wood, as the pony trotted through it, had lost its freshness and ability to delight; the branches of the trees seemed to hang heavy as if they scarcely had the strength to stand up. There was an occasional burst of birdsong and then long silences.

They said their goodbyes at Quay House. Philip shook hands solemnly with Sophie and Maria, but when he bent to Emma she flung her arms round his neck and hugged him. 'Thank you for a lovely day.'

Her sisters looked shocked, but Aunt Jude smiled indulgently, put her hands on Emma's shoulders and drew her back. 'We must think up another excursion soon, Mr Steer,' she said, and marshalling the children before her began to walk towards the house.

Isobel held out her hand to Philip. 'Goodbye, Mr Steer.'

His fingers were very light, very soft; they seemed to hold hers without even touching them. Philip struggled to find something appropriate to say but, failing, bent quickly over Isobel's hand and turned away.

Isobel felt that she floated rather than walked down the garden path. She paused in the doorway, listening to the hubbub in the hall, meditatively stroking her hand with one finger. Nancy was helping Aunt Jude off with her wraps and the little girls were besieging them both with exclamations of delight about the picnic. Isobel could still feel the pressure of Philip's fingers against her own, the moment when his lips had touched the back of her hand; but *had* they touched her, or had they merely hovered above her fingers? Was it only that she had wanted to feel them touch her?

'I think Mr Steer is divine,' breathed Sophie.

'That will do, Sophie,' said her mother sharply.

'Oh, ma'am, there's a letter come for you.'

Nancy picked up a small silver tray with an envelope on it.

'Mama, who is it from?' Sophie bounced up to her.

Isobel just held the letter in her hands. The writing was unmistakable. 'From Papa,' she said quietly.

'Come, girls,' said Aunt Jude quickly, 'upstairs and change your clothes.'

From the half-landing she turned to smile fondly at her niece, whom she imagined wished to be alone with her letter. But Isobel had already vanished into the drawing room.

She stood at the French windows, turning the envelope over and over in her hands. She had forgotten him. She stared at her faint reflection in the clear glass. Her husband's image was no more substantial than that. If she broke open the envelope and unfolded the sheet of paper that would be inside it his face would grow clearer, and as she read his letter his voice would sound louder and louder.

'Why has this come now?' she thought angrily. 'Why has it come to spoil such a lovely day?' And her anger frightened her. If only she could just tear it in half, unopened, and pretend it had never come. But she had a duty to open it. It was from her husband. Besides, they had all seen it. She pulled at one corner of the flap of the envelope, but the paper was so thick and the glue so efficient that for a moment it resisted her fingers. Finally, it tore, a long, jagged edge. She had, fleetingly, an image of Philip's face, staring at her wide-eyed and curious, with the special look she called his artist's eye, a look that seemed to take in everything with great seriousness.

London, June 10th, 1887

My dear,

I was glad to have news of your safe arrival at Walberswick and to hear that both yourself and the children find the place agreeable. It is to be hoped that by now your Aunt's obligations to her sick friend are ended, that her family obligations have prevailed and that she is now installed with you.

Mama is no better. Her condition fluctuates almost daily and is, the doctors say, unlikely to improve. Much as I regret our separation, I feel it my duty to stay with her in town. My brother says that he is unable to come up and visit her at all this month, as his wife expects their fourth child. As Mama may possibly not last longer than the summer, my presence is all the more timely – and his absence the more surprising.

Business, too, detains me, with more activity than is usual for the summer. Absurd talk in the Market is that the Queen's Jubilee is the reason. It is certainly the reason for a great deal of activity in the capital and a great expenditure of public money. Ceremonial arches and memorials are being constructed, public buildings cleaned and stands will soon be erected all along the royal route. London will be disagreeably packed with sightseers and your situation in the calm of the countryside will be much envied. Of course, if you insist on coming up to town for the Procession, then I shall try to hire you a stand, though I believe almost all have been taken despite their exorbitant prices. We have, of course, a Company stand, but in that I must play host to important clients.

I shall try to join you and the children for the first or second week-end in July. Until then, my love to yourself and the children and my respects to your aunt.

Yours as always,
Reginald.

Isobel folded the letter very carefully along its crease. She looked out into the gardens. At the far end of the lawn, against the walls, hung great swathes of blue flowers, as blue as the sky above them. She stared at them, wishing she were one of them – unfeeling, unhearing, unseeing. It was evident from the letter that Reginald wanted to see her as little as she wanted to see him. She was not, after all, his first concern. What was she? Her mind cast around, blankly, numbly, not knowing what to look for – nor what it might find. Such questions were not asked. One did not question . . . The blue flowers swung gently in a sudden breeze. And she realised bitterly that her wish had already been granted long ago: to him she was no more than a flower. A flower to grace his house, an object among other objects, kept, like all his objects, for his glory – no, no, it was worse than that, it was not his glory. She had been feeling her way through unfamiliar territory cautiously, but now the solution came to her in a rush. It was not that he delighted in these objects for themselves; he kept them because they were necessary, necessary means to an end. They were wealth and they would, properly displayed, attract more wealth. It was the one thing he cared about, drily, avidly — money. It was the driving force of his life. He fed her, clothed her, set her at the head of his table, smiled at her to make her smile at his guests . . . all for money.

She felt a rising scream of hysteria and leant against the window as though to press it back into her. It subsided finally, leaving her shaking and empty. She opened her eyes again and felt how cool the glass was against her forehead. Unlike her, he knew what he wanted. It filled his every thought. His letter was money, all through. The Jubilee of the dear old Queen was money wasted. The absence of his brother from the bedside of his dying mother was not filial disregard, but money jeopardised. What was love for a wife and an unborn child compared with the possible loss of an inheritance? He knew better, he stayed in London and paid court to an old woman he cared nothing for — let his wife languish in some coastal village! Money was a fickle thing, like love. It could be lost at any moment. It needed nurturing, guarding, guiding right up to the time when one could grasp its full reward, and even then, at the supreme moment, it might just trickle away through one's fingers.

'Money!' She spat the word out with all the distaste of centuries of money behind her, so solidly behind her that it never needed to be talked about. It was just there in the parkland and the outlying farms and the old house and the dark portraits that had followed her up the stairs to bed every night. To be betrayed for money by . . . by . . . such a parvenu! She closed her eyes. 'I will not cry,' she whispered to herself between clenched teeth. She tightened her fist around the letter and heard the paper crackle in her hand.

'Mama!'

She opened her eyes quickly and the blue flowers at the bottom of the garden swam in a mist of tears. She straightened the crumpled paper and bent her head as though she were reading it.

'What?' She replied without turning round.

'How is Papa?'

Emma stood by the piano holding Aunt Jude's hand. It was too irritating that Mama would not look round and see her new dress.

'What does he say?' clamoured Maria again.

'That . . . that Granny is ill . . . and that he is busy and that he sends you his – love.'

Mama's voice sounded odd. Very high-pitched and fast.

'When is he coming down?' pestered Sophie.

'Next month.'

Still Mama did not turn round.

'*Next* month!' Sophie was scathing.

Emma could stand it no longer. 'Mama! We've got our new striped dresses on for dinner!'

Mama did turn round then. 'So you have.' And she smiled at them all with a smile that twisted up her mouth and left her eyes blank.

Chapter Seven

Emma sat in front of Philip and dug in the sand with her hands to make a castle. She began with a wide base around which she dug a ditch, piling up the sand from it to form the walls.

'Mama got a letter from Papa last night.'

It was as if she'd thrown sand in his face. The sea was blotted out for a second as his paintbrush stopped in mid-air. Ever since yesterday he had floated in a daze, walking in a bemused way through a light fog of happiness. A kind of tip-toeing certainty, an almost-sureness that perhaps she, too, loved . . . But Emma brought him face to face with reality. *Mama* had a letter from *Papa*. It was like a stupid sentence out of a French grammar. As stupid as his ridiculous ideas that she might love him after all, or that it might be permissible for him to love her. There was a giant shadow always between them. Papa!

What was her husband like? Philip couldn't conceive that she could possibly love him. Why was she spending the summer alone if they loved each other? 'If she were mine,' he thought wildly, 'I wouldn't be separated from her for a moment.' He looked down at Emma, calmly building her castle, as though she expected no reply from him. She would know. He had only to ask her. Ever since yesterday, Philip had ceased to think of Isobel as being married, as if her motherhood were by some divine act of connection rather than birth. As if the three children had been lent to her to give her an aura of tenderness and vulnerability and untouchability. She could be admired, she could be worshipped, she could be desired, but for some reason she could not be touched. He'd never given that reason an image in his mind, never made it a concrete, insurmountable fact – for what was more insurmountable to two lovers than the presence of a husband? He could not even visualise this man who was her husband. But he had only to say to Emma, 'What is your father like?' for the reason to take shape and come alive. For the foolishness and pointlessness of his feelings for Isobel to become exposed. The illusion that he could love her and she might love him would be shattered. And once this image confronted Philip, then Philip's relation to Isobel would crumble. For if Isobel had a husband then she was bound to him at least by her duty as a wife, at worst because she loved him.

Philip sat immobilised by the question that twitched in his head, that seemed to shout out so loud in the stillness of his thoughts that he half expected Emma to look up from her sandcastle and answer it. Once asked and once answered things would not be the same. He could not exist in a fog of ignorance weaving dreams whose insubstantiality seemed not at all out of place in such a mist. Knowledge would blow the fog away. The very irrevocability tempted him. A desire to call up this spectre and see if his image really did make everything fall apart jostled and nagged at him like a little demon dancing in wild excitement at the possibility of destruction. It conjured up fleeting memories of the comfort of life without passion, of his studio, his work, his friends, the unruffled pattern of his daily life where nothing was allowed to distract or compete with his painting. Why bother with unrequited love? He'd seen his friends fall into that trap and submerge themselves in misery as though in a pool of honey.

In front of him, Emma sat back on her heels and contemplated the half-built castle with a self-satisfied smile. Then she looked up and caught Philip's gaze.

'I'm going to build it twice as big as this.' And she bent forward again, scrabbling sand out of the moat as fast as a dog digging for a bone.

'I'm not in misery,' thought Philip. 'Why ask questions that can only shatter the happiness we all have? Everything is perfectly correct. If it were not, it would be commented on. Isobel's aunt would disapprove. Isobel herself would not welcome me if my attentions were unwanted.'

The fact that he could not express the true extent of his feelings to Isobel gave them an extra dimension of pleasure, a certain delicious pain, a holding back and a longing that would not be fulfilled. Love, like that, could last for ever. He saw himself and Isobel as two people standing one on either side of a border separating two countries, between them a thin wooden pole, slung across the road as a frontier barrier. That thin wooden pole was all that kept them apart. It was the reason they could never do more than touch hands and gaze into each other's eyes and talk softly of everything except the thing they really wanted to talk about, which was themselves.

While Philip sat on the beach and thought of Isobel, Isobel sat in the vicarage drawing room, thinking of Philip and listening to Aunt Jude and Mrs Round. They were engaged, with the help of the Reverend Round, in discovering mutual acquaintances – that most reassuring of all pastimes – while privately measuring and plotting each other's position on the social graph. In between smiling and nodding sociably at their exclamations over the virtue of this or that good lady of Southwold, Isobel had time to examine the room around her. It was long and low and had something of a tomb-like aspect, though from the windows at one end of the room one could see all the world pass by on the road to the quay, and from the other a vista of marsh and sand-dunes. Nevertheless, one had the feeling of being sunk deep into the ground, as though the house were settling lower and lower into the insubstantiality of the marsh and would in this way be preserved by it. Isobel thought she had read somewhere of excavations into marshes which had revealed animal remains and whole trees perfectly preserved, as they had been in life, by some protective agent within the mud. This drawing room was a perfect candidate for such a burial, being already a shrine. Isobel reflected that when the brown velvet curtains were drawn at night it must become even more tomb-like. All attention would then be focused on the clusters of silver-framed sepia photographs and pale-washed miniatures that crowded the mantelshelves, dressers and occasional tables. In among these huddles of blank faces were glass domes imprisoning bunches of dried flowers, or seascapes of varnished shells. Samplers hung on the walls, pricked out by childish fingers: 'Cicely Round her work, 18th February, 1876', 'Elizabeth Halesworth, 20th June, 1881', 'Louisa Mary Partridge' . . . 'The Lord Is My Shepherd' begun in red wool and finished in green.

'Not a happy choice,' thought Isobel, and wondered which of the cousins and sisters and nieces in the silver photograph frames might be Elizabeth Halesworth or Cicely Rount. But the faces remained nameless and her mind wandered back to Philip.

Isobel had thought of Philip all night. She had lain awake and watched one candle burn itself out, had lit another from the dying remains of the first and watched it, too, gutter down. She lay and listened to the voices in her head: Reginald's and Philip's, unaware of each other — speaking first alternately, then, in the manner of a dream, across each other. Philip's quiet words drowned out by Reginald's assured tone, but listened for all the more tenderly by Isobel for their very softness. Then the voices fell silent and the images began.

Philip appeared, very small and far away, as he did when he stood in the marshes watching for her. In the stillness of the dream, his face seemed slowly to detach itself and float across the ground towards her, growing larger, the features separating themselves and becoming clearer, until the face filled completely the field of her vision and she felt breathless with the tension of holding the image in her head and wanting him to come closer and closer. She could see the very softness of his skin, the way the eyelashes curled — things she could not possibly have known about him. And then his face blotted out all vision, as though it merged with her own, and she could feel her body shudder with long sighs of peace.

Slowly, throughout the night, Isobel recalled him to her, reliving every chance encounter, every glimpse of his watching figure. She recalled the gentleness of him, the shyness and the delicacy. He was so different. Perhaps it was because he was a painter. She had imagined painters to be wild, impulsive, extravagantly dressed, romantic. But he was not like that. She watched the candle-flame quiver in the dark room. She stretched her arms along the sheet slowly, to their fullest extent, and then, smiling to herself in the darkness, gathered them in quickly to her body, hugging herself with a leaping delight. She lay smiling and thoughtless for a while, full of a lazy warmth. Images of all the men who had ever paid court, or pretended to pay court, to her began to drift through her head in a procession. Among these mustachio-twirling cardboard cut-outs appeared her husband, sometimes behaving like all the rest, sometimes standing back a pace, ordering the others on like a bizarre ringmaster. She stared at these images without interest, faintly despising the alien procession as it leered and bowed itself into thin air. On the other side of the room the mirror gleamed darkly, like water.

She thought of the way Philip talked to her: he did not say any of the things her husband's friends said. Where they spoke volubly, he spoke little; where they engineered time alone with her, he was embarrassed by it; where they were bold to ensnare her, he was shy and had enchanted her. She thought of her own tongue-tied silence when they were together. 'It shall never be so again,' she whispered to herself, and saw the candle-flame billow with the force of her breath. 'We must become friends and talk and talk of . . . everything. Never again will there be anyone to whom I shall be able to talk as I will talk with him!' The candle guttered and died, extinguished by the dawn which had crept across the room and covered the sleeping woman's face.

When Isobel's attention returned to Mrs Rount's drawing room, the conversation seemed to be in full flood, and her absent thoughts seemed hardly to have been missed.

'An inspiration!' Aunt Jude was exclaiming.

'An example to us all!' nodded Mrs Rount. 'I quite despair of my own efforts,' she added bitterly, 'when I hear of her committees and organisations, her sewing circles and Bible readings and Friends to Fishermen . . . '

'My dear,' interposed her husband, 'you must not blame yourself, there *are* almost no ladies in Walberswick for you to organise.'

But Mrs Rount had a burning desire to be the redeemer, with a band of like-minded ladies, of the misguided poor, to round them up and fill their heads with piety and common sense. She swept on as though venting long pent-up grievances.

'If there were just one or two other ladies concerned to do their Christian duty, to act as pillars in this outpost.' She shook her head. 'I do what I can for the poor of the parish, but they will not help themselves. They will take whatever anyone gives them – a blanket, cast-off clothes, a bone for soup – anything. But you can give them good advice and they shut their ears to it. They stand there in their miserable hovels with the wind blowing through and the rain leaking in, the whole place filled with smoke from a fire that won't draw, and stare at you as if they didn't understand English. They are a great trial!' She leaned back in her chair as though it were all too exhausting. 'You know what they say about people in these parts? They say that round here people don't live, they linger. And it's true. There's a tradition of poverty here so old it seems immovable, and they won't take any telling from outside. They live like leaves blown by the wind. They cry when it's cold and they laugh and forget they ever cried when the sun shines.'

Mrs Round drew her breath in sharply so that it hissed with disapproval. Aunt Jude nodded slowly and Isobel thought how nice it would be to be a twirling leaf, laughing in the sunshine, dripping tears in the rain. The longer she sat in that sunless room, her hands folded in her lap, listening to Mrs Round's voice whine and scratch like a squeaky pencil against a slate, the more she felt her spirits rise. Reasonlessly. Recklessly. Bursting through the ceiling, not into the rooms above, but into bright blue sky, as though they broke through the whole tight surface of her life and scattered out from where they had been imprisoned. They coloured everything around her with her own delight.

'They won't even be educated!' Mrs Round was beside herself. 'A schoolhouse provided, a teacher, even a law to enforce school attendance. But do they send their children?' She threw up her hands. 'I despair, Round knows.'

The vicar patted her hand. 'My dear, my dear, you forget to mention that it costs a penny to send a child to school. These poor creatures live by the sea. She's a hard mistress, erratic, dangerous, jealous of her plenty. We must not censure them too harshly. We must help them in any way we can — if not to this life then to the life hereafter.'

Still keeping hold of his wife's hand, he turned to Aunt Jude. 'Is that not so, ma'am?'

'It is indeed. We must have compassion.'

The Reverend Round stood up and smiled at Isobel. 'And you, my dear, what do you think of all this?'

Isobel, by now brim full of love, beamed artlessly at them. 'I agree with all of you!' she said, and wondered why they looked so taken aback.

They were fortunately not given long to ponder the unsuitability of Isobel's manner for a discussion on the plight of the poor, before there was a commotion outside, a knock at the door and a scurrying of footsteps down the hall.

'Why, Round, that'll be Mr Smytheson come after all!' Mrs Round leaned forward to Isobel and Aunt Jude with a visibly brightened eye. 'Mr Smytheson, a very dear neighbour of ours, a solicitor you know, with his own firm in Southwold, was thrown several weeks ago from his trap on the Blythburgh Road. He sustained such injuries, we feared for his life. But he has quite recovered, thank the Lord, and today pays his very first visit.'

'It sounds like Philip's friend,' said Aunt Jude to Isobel.

'Oh,' snapped Mrs Round, 'you've met him?'

'No,' smiled Isobel.

Mrs Round gave Isobel a sidelong look. She had never been quite sure she approved of her. But at that moment the door opened and a maid announced, 'Mr Smytheson and Dr Morris.'

Mr Smytheson swung himself forward on his sticks. 'Just to be on the safe side, I've brought my doctor with me. I hope you don't mind, dear Mrs Round?'

At this his companion laughed and shook his head. 'I came not just to keep an eye on my patient, dear lady, but on an errand from my wife.'

Mrs Round introduced them first to Aunt Jude and then to Isobel, and their delight and enthusiasm at the prospect of meeting two new ladies threatened to disrupt the solemnity of the room. Walking-sticks and legs seemed to get tangled up in the narrow passageway between side tables and chairs. Endeavouring to shake hands with Isobel and to beat Dr Morris to the empty seat beside her, Mr Smytheson lost hold of both sticks and was left clinging to Isobel's hand and smiling broadly at his distress. The walking-sticks crashed against a low table, toppling several photographs from their stands and upsetting a vase of waxed flowers. Despite the slithering, Mrs Round's stifled shriek and the clutching of various hands at ornaments and walking-sticks, they got Mr Smytheson on to the sofa next to Isobel, and with reluctance he let go of her hand.

'Are you comfortable?' asked Dr Morris, archly. 'Shall we find you another cushion for your back?'

Mr Smytheson beamed up at him smugly. 'No thank you, dear physician. I am most comfortable, most comfortable.' He turned to wink at Isobel and found the movement hurt his ribs. 'Ah, Morris, could you just turn me a little, so that I can face Mrs Heatherington as I talk to her?'

The doctor gave him his arm and Smytheson shuffled slightly to the right. 'Just so, just so. I am a little stiff, my dear, on account of fallin' out of my chaise and bruisin' every one of my ribs. Now I can see both yourself and your good aunt.' He nodded gaily across the room to Aunt Jude and in doing so caught sight of the disturbed look on Mrs Rount's face.

'You see, my dear Mrs Rount, what a tiresome thing it is to invite invalids to take tea with one. But you couldn't have devised a faster way to recovery than invitin' me to share the company of two such charmin' ladies.'

'Well, I declare!' Mrs Rount was quite put out by the commotion and the levity. 'I think we shall have tea. Rount, will you ring?'

'Certainly, my dear, certainly.' The vicar seemed caught mid-way between his natural gregariousness and desire to join in the sparring flirtations of the two men and the sombre aspect of his wife's decorum.

Dr Morris took a chair next to Aunt Jude. 'May I have the pleasure of sitting next to you?'

She gave him one of her most glittering smiles. 'I should be honoured, Dr Morris.'

For a moment, Mr Smytheson stared at them both as though wondering if he had miscalculated, and whether he shouldn't change places. But he turned instantly to Isobel as if determined to outshine the other pair.

'I have been longin' to meet you,' he said, smiling at her coyly in full view of the company.

'Indeed,' replied Isobel, trying not to laugh. It seemed as though this vivacious old man was possessed of spirits as soaring and light as her own. She hardly wondered whether he was in fact as delightful as she found him, or whether it was just that she found everything suddenly delightful.

'Yes,' continued Mr Smytheson, 'for days and days. Ever since my young friend Philip Steer first told me of you.'

It is one thing to be in a good-humoured dream when you think no one can guess why. It is quite another to imagine that your secret has been guessed. Isobel was sure her cheeks were flushed, that she smiled too much and that everyone in the room had heard Philip's name mentioned. But the moment the shock had passed, pleasure followed, both at the sound of his name and at the thought that he had talked of her to this old man. And then came the rush of longing to hear of what he had said and how he had looked and when all this had taken place. She was prevented from revealing herself completely only by the entry of the tea-tray.

Over tea, Dr Morris remembered why he had come there in the first place. 'Colonel Miles's wife and Mrs Morris have decided that we should have festivities in Dunwich to mark the Jubilee of Queen Victoria, something for the whole parish to join in. And so they have organised a Jubilee Fête and detailed me to invite yourself and the Reverend Rount.' He turned to Aunt Jude. 'I am quite sure that if my wife had also made the acquaintance of you and your niece, she would have insisted that you and Mrs Heatherington should do us the honour of being present too. May I insist on her behalf?'

Aunt Jude smiled indulgently. 'I'm sure we should be delighted, shouldn't we, Isobel.'

'Indeed.'

'When is it to be?'

'Next Wednesday, the 29th of June, the day on which the Queen is to hold a Garden Party herself at Buckingham Palace.'

'Won't you be going up to join your husband in London?' interposed Mrs Rount spitefully. 'I'm sure I shouldn't care to miss the opportunity to attend all the jollifications, the balls and the processions.'

'Alas, my husband doesn't care for processions and public festivities. He has written to me complaining how London is being transformed by garlands and plaques and stands and notices. No, he stays up in London to keep company with his mother, who is ill, and to attend to his business.'

'Well,' thought Mrs Rount, 'that is one possible explanation,' and disliked Isobel all the more for her apparent unconcern at this temporary widowhood.

'Then you will say yes?' smiled the doctor.

'I should be delighted to join you and I know my young daughters will be thrilled.'

'You have young daughters?' echoed Dr Morris.

'Yes, three.'

'Wonderful!' exclaimed Mr Smytheson. 'We can all play Papa.'

Isobel blushed.

'We are to have an ox roast, and rural sports, and a band, and country dancing, and a tableau – I lose track of the entertainments planned. Each day my wife seems to announce a new one.'

'We shall be quite a party,' said the Reverend Rount, rubbing his hands together. 'We shall be seven, no eight, from Walberswick.'

'I should like to make it nine,' announced Mr Smytheson.

'My dear fellow!' exclaimed the vicar. 'I wouldn't dream of not including you – you're already counted in.'

'No, I ask on behalf of a young friend of mine.' Mr Smytheson paused. 'You all know him, with the exception of Dr Morris: Steer, the young painter.'

'Oh, yes, young Philip Steer, good idea, Smytheson. You think he would enjoy a jaunt like this?' asked the vicar.

'I'm sure he would,' beamed Aunt Jude. 'He escorted us on a most delightful picnic the other day.' She turned to Mrs Rount. 'To Foxburrow Wood, so pretty. The children even found some late bluebells.' And they began discussing places of beauty in the local countryside.

'I should be delighted for Mr Steer to come,' said Dr Morris. 'Perfect thing for a painter, a country fête.'

The three men fell to sorting out the necessary transport to get eight people over to Dunwich, how long it would take, and what provision they should make for rain, or a horse casting a shoe.

It was not quite by chance that Philip and Isobel met a couple of evenings later as she took her promenade to the pier with her children and stood to watch the evening sunlight over the sea. Seeing that her horizon-gazing had become customary, Philip had several times tried to pluck up the courage to join them, hovering on the quay below the pier, looking seawards up at them and then turning away in confusion. This particular evening, he forced himself to walk on across the Hard, through the groups of fishermen, towards the pier, talking to himself all the time. It was not, he told himself, improper to stroll upon the quay at evening, nor to walk out, for a better view of the sea, along the pier. It was the done thing in Walberswick, when there was any company to do it with. Nor could it be considered, on meeting a lady of one's acquaintance, improper to raise one's hat, bid her 'good evening' and make some comment on the beauty of the scene.

He felt the palms of his hands sticky with sweat. He was on the pier now. She stood, as always, at the far end, gazing out to sea, her back to him. There was an awful directness in the path he had to take to reach her. Emma, Sophie and Maria, racing the length of the pier and shrieking, in some game of tag, unnerved him so much that he halted as they dashed past and circled behind him, as though to cut off his retreat. He went on and they left him alone. Finally, he reached the wooden rail at the end of the pier, where Isobel stood.

'Good evening,' he said, in a strangled voice that was hardly more than a whisper.

But she heard it. 'Good evening.' She turned towards him without the least trace of surprise in her face or her voice, as though she had been expecting him.

'I hope I don't disturb you . . . I didn't see you until I was on the pier and then . . . you seemed so deep in thought . . . '

'Not deep thoughts. I was thinking about the Jubilee celebrations to be held in Dunwich. Are you coming?' asked Isobel.

'I feel very honoured,' smiled Philip. 'It seems to have been the one question on everybody's lips for the past few days. Mr Smytheson phrased it in such a way that I was obliged to accept, and when Mrs Rount asked me it was clear she hoped I'd refuse.'

Isobel laughed softly and turned to watch her children. They were leapfrogging the bollards now, one after the other, all down the centre of the pier.

'Mrs Rount would not approve,' murmured Philip.

'No.' Isobel smiled to herself, a little curling smile, like a small wave breaking over the calm line of her profile. Philip wanted to make her turn to him so that he could have her smile all to himself.

'Did you like Mr Smytheson?' he asked.

'Yes, very much.' She glanced at Philip, but couldn't bring herself to explain how very fond she was of the old man because he talked to her of Philip and told her how Philip talked to him of her – and because he was, in thought, if not in practice, their messenger long before they were aware that they needed one.

'He has great charm,' she added.

'He thought so of you too,' Philip replied.

Isobel turned and leaned on the railings, looking out to sea. 'It's so lovely here in the early evening. The sea seems to make everything peaceful, even when the waves are rough. I hate this hour or so between the end of tea and dressing for dinner. It always seems so melancholy. One feels drained of energy, drained of conversation, as though one has done everything and said everything one wanted to say during the day, but not yet caught the animation of the evening. It seems to be a time when the countryside is beautifully and calmly composing itself for sleep, when nature is at its most perfect – but it only makes me feel out of step with it: ragged, lost, dancing out of time. Do you ever feel that way, Mr Steer, or is one of the rewards of being a painter the fact that one is always in tune with nature?' She went on before he could answer her. 'Somehow, standing here, with the sea all around me, just looking out into it, quite calms that ragged feeling and soothes the melancholy. Few other people seem to come out here at this hour.'

'I've never liked to disturb you before,' began Philip.

She turned to him then, as though she wanted to say something, but could not find the courage or the words, and he in turn could not finish his own sentence. They sensed each other's distress and both saw how it broke the bounds of propriety.

'My aunt,' said Isobel loudly into the silence, 'is beside herself with curiosity about your painting. She is eager to see some of it, and so am I, if it wouldn't be too much trouble. Emma says you've drawn her.'

'Just a sketch.'

'We'd love to see it.'

'Perhaps you would allow me to sketch you again?'

'Just here?'

'If you like.'

'Yes, here; like this, staring out to sea, so that when I go back to London it will remind . . . ' Her voice trailed away.

This time Philip came to the rescue. 'I can't do it right now,

I'm afraid, I left my things in my room; just came down here to stretch my legs. I've been sitting in a cornfield all afternoon.'

'A cornfield?' She laughed. 'That doesn't sound very grand or artistic!'

'All good drawing practice.' Philip grinned.

She put her head on one side. 'Do you know, I've never met an artist before.'

He laughed, proud of her innocent admiration. 'Well . . . '

'Mama, Mama!' There were shouts from the other end of the pier.

'Coming!' she called back. And to him, 'I must go.' She held out her hand, smiling. 'Shall I stand for my portrait just here tomorrow evening?'

'Yes.' He bent over her fingers.

She moved quickly away and then turned back to him, shading her eyes with one gloved hand. 'Oh, and tea at Quay House the day after tomorrow with some of your drawings?'

He nodded. And then she left, walking quickly away down the pier, gathering her children in one by one as she went, until they turned in a straggling line across the shingle at the end of the pier and disappeared between the black, tarred fishermen's huts.

Philip turned back to the sea, leaning out over the rail as she had done, as though looking for the peace that she had found in the forming and re-forming of the waves. But the water glittered with the lowering sun, sharp stabs of bright light shivering and breaking the placid surface of the water, so that he found no calming of the clamour Isobel provoked in him.

Chapter Eight

The subject of Queen Victoria's Golden Jubilee engrossed them all for the remainder of the week. It was a time bound up in Emma's mind for years to come with the remembrance, not of feverish excitement, but of a slight and mounting feeling of dread. Sophie and Maria fed on any scrap of information relating to the Jubilee that they could scavenge, and were beside themselves for news from London. They were completely caught up in the devotional fervour, the torrent of self-satisfaction that swept England, the love that flowed from the hearts of thousands of subjects to engrave and donate their moment of largesse in honour of their queen.

When Philip climbed on to the pier a few evenings later he was met, half-way along, by a galloping procession: Emma and Maria with makeshift reins around their waists, being driven on by an imperious Sophie.

'Playing horses?' he inquired genially.

Sophie tossed her head and drove on without replying.

'Not playing horses,' he remarked, as he came level with Isobel.

She smiled. 'We are being Queen Victoria. The trouble is we cannot all be Queen Victoria at the same time.' She paused, looking back at her children.

'How are you?' asked Philip in a low voice.

'I'm well,' she answered quietly. They began to walk slowly towards the end of the pier. 'At first we were delighted that they had found a new game. Now we fear they have merely discovered a new thing to squabble about. Mr Smytheson has begun to join us for tea in the afternoon, and kindly reads to the girls the latest bulletin on the Jubilee celebrations from his *Times*. Since then they have become enthralled and can talk of little else.'

'Will Smytheson come with us to Blythburgh Church tomorrow?'

'In the chaise?' Isobel looked at him with arched eyebrows. 'His ribs are scarcely mended from his accident.'

'Of course, I had forgotten. It will be just us, then.'

'Just all six of us,' added Isobel ruefully.

After all his efforts merely to become acquainted with this woman, the idea of being invited to spend an afternoon with her was bliss: he did not care whether there would be six of them in the party, or a hundred. He could talk to her, be close enough to touch her, look up and see her near him, and feel proud, if strangers passed them, to be one of her company.

In those wide, unfettered landscapes of East Anglia, where the majesty of sky takes precedence over all else, one can quite forget that the earth has any importance at all. One can become totally enslaved by the capricious dancing of a cloud. So it was with Emma as they drove over the heath the following afternoon towards Blythburgh. She leaned back in her seat and watched the sun blotted out and then suddenly reappearing bright as before as huge black shadows passed above her. It was like an army thundering at full gallop over her head. Below, smaller clouds raced in hypnotic swirls and wisps like teasing ghosts, making themselves into forms that dissolved as soon as Emma put a name to them, drawing her after them into their chameleon-like existence until she felt she had no shape or form herself and was up there with them, streaming out along the wind. She felt as if the sky had changed places with the sea, and she was sailing through it, faster and faster, the white, cloud-like sails billowing out around her.

By the time they got to Blythburgh Church, she was so dazed that the earth seemed still to be spinning, and the sky to be sailing on past her. The towering bulk of the church before her seemed like a huge ship, berthed in the marshes. The party gathered outside the main door of the church, whose panels had weathered to a pale, salt-grained colour which gave it an exhausted look, as though it had withstood much. There was a great rearranging of hats, retying of ribbons, straightening of dresses and smoothing of gloves.

'Will there be a service?' asked Emma, who had thought that the excursion was to be just like Foxburrow Wood, without the picnic tea.

'No, dear,' replied Aunt Jude, 'we've come to admire the architecture,' and took firm hold of one of Emma's hands.

Mr Steer started telling them about the church, pointing at it and making shapes in the air with his hands. But Emma's attention was distracted by Sophie, who had insisted on bringing her reticule with her. In fact, she had insisted on changing her clothes several times before Mama had got quite cross with her and told her to stop being so vain, or they would have to leave without her. She had been unusually quiet all the way over in the chaise, holding herself very straight and staring directly in front of her, but Emma had merely assumed that she was sulking. Now she was fascinated to see Sophie draw from her reticule a prayer-book.

She leaned forward. 'There isn't going to be a service, you know. Aunt Jude said so.'

Sophie stared at her haughtily. 'Then I shall pray,' she replied coldly, and clasping her prayer-book she turned her eyes to heaven, which was in the general direction towards which Mr Steer waved his arms.

They went inside, tiptoeing in a respectful line.

It was so big, it wasn't like a church at all. And yet it wasn't like anywhere that Emma had ever seen before. Light poured into the vast, white space from huge windows set high up, near the roof. They stood in attentive groups while Mr Steer pointed out various features of interest. They craned their necks to see the heads carved at the top of the soaring colonnades that supported the roof. They clustered about round brasses set into the floor, inspected the font and admired the marble urns, carved for the immortal memory of the dear departed, in niches along the walls. They clattered and rustled thoroughly over every inch of the great nave. Mr Steer spoke all the time in the low voice adults use when they are in church, so that Emma missed much of what he said, found her mind wandering and began to lag behind. Everyone else, she observed, was rapt with attention. Aunt Jude, her mouth slightly open, nodded and smiled at each new wonder, beaming encouragingly at Maria, who now stood by her side. Sophie, still clutching her prayer-book, stared at everything with an unchanging expression of cold piety. Mama, however, thought Emma, stared more at Mr Steer than at the church, and he, in his turn, seemed to direct most of his discourse towards her, only now and then shifting his gaze to one of the others, as if suddenly recollecting himself. He seemed not to be taking any notice of Emma at all.

The party returned to the back of the nave, close to the door where they had come in, and stood together in a group looking down at the base of the wall. Dawdling in the midst of the wide space between the back of the pews and the back of the church, Emma was struck by the irreverent thought that the space was so huge that it was more like a room for dancing in, with all the pews looking as if they had been pushed to the front out of the way. She could imagine the place where she stood full of gossiping, flirting ladies and gentlemen in beautiful, ornate clothes.

'Emma!'

'Come on, dear, you're missing it.'

They parted to let her in, looking at her with strange, gloating smiles.

'What do you think it is?' asked Mr Steer.

At the foot of the wall was an iron grille, and behind that a curious, tomb-like space hollowed out from the thickness of the wall, barely high enough for Emma to stand upright in. The image of gay ladies paled before the dread that this cage aroused in her. She looked up bemused, at all their faces watching her, their looks of know-and-won't-tell. She felt almost as if the cage were for her, that they might put her in it as a joke, and then leave her . . .

'Don't you know?'

Even Aunt Jude was a party to it. Emma shook her head.

'It's a priest's hole,' announced Mr Steer, and a light sigh of satisfaction seemed to issue from the assembled company at the imparting of this knowledge.

'Priests were shut up in these holes for weeks or months at a time to escape detection by Cromwell's men.'

'I wonder how many died in there,' said Sophie with pious relish.

Emma shrank back against her mother. 'I want to go home now,' she whispered urgently. But her mother disengaged herself with a little, gay laugh and moved away.

'Come,' she said over her shoulder to no one in particular, and Mr Steer followed her. They wandered off together across the wide dancing space.

Emma turned to her aunt. 'I don't like it here.' She felt close to tears.

'Nonsense, dear. We haven't seen half of everything yet.'

Sophie came up and slid her arm through her aunt's. 'I think I'd like to pray for a little, Aunt,' she said superciliously.

'Come and say a prayer, Emma,' whispered Aunt Jude, as though inviting her to take a hand at whist.

Emma pulled away. 'I want to go outside.'

'Don't go outside on your own,' replied Aunt Jude, sailing off with Sophie.

Emma stood very still on the flagstones of the nave and watched how, at the other end of the church, Mama's long skirts swayed and pressed themselves against Mr Steer's legs as she walked. Then they vanished suddenly behind a pillar, and Emma ran outside into the churchyard.

She stood on the gravel path in front of the porch, basking in the warm ordinariness of the world, gulping in the summer air, as though she had been momentarily suffocated by some unidentifiable fear. It was very quiet. She stood in the sunshine for what seemed a long time and then wandered off along the path to see where it led. She walked close to the church, trailing one finger against the wall, which had been set with patterns of flints, so that her finger bumped from one smooth pebble to the next. There were flints on pillars that ran out at a low angle from the wall, too, set in patterns of black and white, lozenges and diamonds carefully cut and placed.

'Like a chequer-board,' thought Emma, running her fore-finger from square to square, counting out moves under her breath. Absorbed by these child-sized gaming tables set at such regular intervals along the length of the church, she temporarily forgot her fear. She searched in the grass for stones to use as counters, but the angle of the 'board' was too steep and they always rolled off. Suddenly, the guilty thought struck her that perhaps God had made the stones fall off, as punishment for playing such irreverent games. Leaning on one of the buttresses, she looked quickly up into the sky to see if she were being watched. Silhouetted against the blue, where the top of the wall ended and the roof of the church sloped away, stone eyes stared back at her blindly, set in faces that were not human. Emma felt a tickling, crawling frisson, a pleasurable horror, like the probing of confused and nameless ancient fears. The faces above her shared a terror far worse, their expressions arrested at some moment of supreme horror, their mouths opened in screams of pain. Emma took a step backwards and craned her neck to hear them. But the centuries had carried off their howls and mingled them with countless others, so that all that remained was the ancient silence to trouble and provoke her. She shuffled along the gravel path to get a better view of the faces, her head arched to the sky.

Foxes' heads, with snarling teeth and long tongues, goblins' heads, cats' heads with small round ears and human features, rose heads and angels' heads, all curls and starched ruffs, expressionless among the rictuses of agony around them. Angels that did not heed the turbulence of life on earth, nor the joy of heaven above them, nor the evil that stalked between earth and heaven. 'The angels,' whispered Emma in a sudden comprehension of the possible loneliness of mankind, 'don't care!' And the sense of disquiet, of stray evil, that seemed to haunt the church, returned.

It was at this point that Emma, having rounded the apse of the church, found herself in front of a small door set deep into the wall, almost hidden from view by the shadow of a flying buttress. It was slightly ajar, and the dank air which seeped out of its darkness made Emma draw back into the sunlight, almost tripping over a stone slab raised out of the paved path which led away from the door. She stared at the slab and felt the same frisson of curiosity that the gargoyles had inspired. The church seemed attended by things more unearthly than heavenly, more mysterious than mystical. She bent down and traced with her finger the circle that was engraved upon the stone. Around the circle were markings – figures, numbers. Diagonal lines ran from the centre of the circle like the rays of the sun, dividing it off into segments. Some of the marks were very faint, as though countless fingers had traced their way across its face. She was a magician, and this was her magic stone; it could grant her every prayer. She began to whisper, 'Abracadabra, abracadabra . . . ', and to run her finger round the engraved face of the circle so that its shadow crossed and recrossed the ancient markings. The whispering became an unidentifiable hiss of breath in her ears and her finger flew faster and faster

94

until the rough surface burned her skin. And then she heard, unmistakably, a low laugh. It came from the open doorway. Emma's finger froze. It was Mama's laugh. And Mama's skirt which showed a line of white in the darkness. It was Mama who laughed again, very low. But Emma did not know which one of them it was who then shut the door.

It felt suddenly cold kneeling outside, there on the path. She looked down at where her finger lay on the stone and pressed it savagely into the surface, so that the lines bit into her skin. 'Take him away,' she hissed. 'Take him away!' and her face contorted with fear.

'Emma, Emma!'

From the church porch her sisters were calling her, their voices coming nearer. Emma scrambled to her feet. She wasn't going to share the magic stone with anyone. She appeared suddenly from behind one of the stone buttresses further down the church and startled them.

Maria stared at her suspiciously. 'Where have you been?'

'Nowhere.'

'Aunt Jude said you weren't to go outside.'

Emma shrugged her shoulders and looked away.

Chapter Nine

The day of the Jubilee fête grew nearer, and the Jubilee frenzy that reigned in Quay House became intense. The delights of the beach paled for Sophie and Maria in comparison with Mr Smytheson's daily visits with his newspaper. Like diminutive history dons they would nod dreamily with pleasure as the ancient titles of Europe's monarchy fell with hyphenated richness on their ears. They would interrupt suddenly as particular passages in Mr Smytheson's recitations struck them with special force, and digress with passion on such matters as the fortune of Princess Victoria of Schleswig-Holstein to be driving with Prince Alfred of Edinburgh in the very first carriage of the Queen's procession to Westminster Abbey for the Jubilee service. Or the vision of the Princess of Wales, with her ladies-in-waiting, nobly distributing prizes at a London orphanage to mark the Jubilee. Mr Smytheson was aware on these occasions that though he could be sure of Sophie and Maria's attention, he usually failed to break through the web of abstraction in which Emma seemed increasingly to be tangled. He would look up from time to time from his reading and see her staring at him, not with the rapt attention of her sisters, but in a questioning, mazed sort of way, as though trying to see through skin and bone to what he really was, unable to trust to ordinary sight.

In this way, they learned of the arrivals of all the crowned heads of Europe and of the plenipotentiaries of the loyal colonies; of the arrangements in the Abbey and the magnificent decorations, public and private, that lined the streets of London. It became the custom, when the day's reading from *The Times* was over, for Sophie and Maria to drag Emma with them to enact the scene they had just heard, reappearing in the garden festooned with lengths of butter muslin and discarded curtaining. Mr Smytheson would watch them out of the corner of his eye as he chatted with Isobel and her aunt, drawn to them by the eerie impression they made — something to do with the glass doors between himself and them that allowed him to witness their private game, to see the gesticulation but not to hear the obvious arguments. Watching them was like having the words he had just read re-run through his brain at different speeds, as in a dream, events being heightened out of all proportion, split seconds drawn into unbearable infinity, words pouring from mouths in silence.

Sophie and Maria, at least, were quite carried away by the game. Emma was not. She appeared to be given a series of minor parts, about which she sometimes remonstrated, sometimes sulked, ending up acting her role with an enthusiasm which burnt itself into apathy within a few minutes. It was almost as if she did not really know what was required of her. Eventually she would sidle off into the shadow of a large magnolia bush that grew close to the terrace, and pluck at its leaves, glancing frequently with vague anxiety through the French windows at the silhouette of her mother.

Philip, having learned of Mr Smytheson's visits to Quay House, seized the opportunity to accompany him and took great pleasure in feeling himself accepted as a friend of the family. Aunt Jude was delighted to have established 'afternoons' in such a desolate place as Walberswick, and congratulated herself that she had secured all the eligible bachelors in the village. Their little 'salon' provoked sour mutterings from the vicar's wife, who felt excluded. Neither was it unnoticed by the villagers, and 'them goings-about' and 'them teas' were the subject of much gossip. Aunt Jude, prey to her good intentions, saw nothing improper in the attentions of her new friends. If Mrs Rount had ever dared to suggest that their little circle might be over-familiar, 'Tut, tut, Mrs Rount,' she might have said, 'blessed are the pure in heart . . . ' For her darlings were all, she was quite convinced, possessed of the purest of hearts. Little Emma, to be sure, was a trifle cast-down and mopish these days, but a prettier picture of innocence and patriotic devotion than her great-nieces one could not imagine. And then there was Isobel, her favourite niece: what angel could be purer than Isobel!

Isobel felt herself to be in torment. When she had first told Philip of Smytheson's visits, it was to provoke him into coming too, thereby further declaring his hand. But she discovered that having him in her house for any length of time frightened her. It was not what he said or did that alarmed her; it was his presence. The soft ease of his body, which filled so comfortably the armchair he lay in; the tapering fingers she longed to reach out and touch, draped calmly along the arm of the chair. She could touch them only briefly, on his arrival and departure, a fleeting second of a touch that she craved for the rest of the afternoon. Their looks and smiles and conversations, while Aunt Jude and Mr Smytheson were engaged on other topics, were tantalising shadows of how they might have talked to each other had they been truly alone. Far from having pushed Philip into showing his hand, she was now tortured by the fact that he would not show it. She heaped unspoken reproaches on him because he made no effort to engineer even a few seconds alone with her, took no pretexts to bend over her or inadvertently brush his arm against hers, or to allow the tips of his fingers to touch hers in what might seem accidental carelessness. He was content, or so he seemed – content just to be in the same room with her, content that the others should be constantly in their way. When the children left the room for their dressing-up games, something in Isobel's head screamed at her aunt to leave too, and take Mr Smytheson with her. But her aunt, fortunately, heard nothing of the nightmare howling of Isobel's passion and sat on in the drawing room, holding court, till the two men reluctantly took their leave.

Philip was content, happily, comfortably content – until he was alone in his room at 'The Anchor', and then the lost opportunities of his visits assailed him. In the beginning he had longed only to catch a glimpse of her, then to become acquainted with her; but these states of bliss once achieved became dull, outshone by new desires. All the same, he could not see how he could prolong their moments of private conversation or those seconds when they stood close together, temporarily ignored by the others in the busyness of arrivals or departures, without attracting notice, without courting impropriety or incurring the censure of Aunt Jude.

The following Monday, Queen Victoria, accompanied by her children and grandchildren from all the royal courts of Europe, left Windsor Castle to travel by train to London in preparation for the Jubilee the next day. All over England anticipation mounted. Beacon fires were stacked, fireworks set up, fêtes, parties and balls organised. In Walberswick, the party that was to attend the fête in Dunwich was invited to tea at Quay House. The day was so hot that Isobel had the servants carry everything outside, and the informality of taking tea on the lawn added to the general feeling of excitement.

'Just think,' exclaimed Maria at one point, leaping up from the grass and startling Mrs Rount. 'Just think, Queen Victoria is on a railway train right now.'

And they all thought, momentarily, of the deification of the 3.42 from Reading to London, with so many royal personages inside it.

'Shall we go to Dunwich tomorrow by train?' asked Emma.

'We could, we could,' mused Mr Smytheson. 'I had not thought of that.'

'Ah, no,' interposed the vicar, one plump finger squeezed through the delicate handle of his teacup. 'We could not, I fear. The local line is closed, as the day is a public holiday. Besides, my dear Miss Heatherington, we have arranged for two chaises to carry us. We shouldn't like to disappoint. It will, I assure you, be more fun under our own steam. We can go when we please and leave when we please. All we have to settle is who should sit where.'

As if at a signal, all other conversation ceased. Teacups were put down and sandwiches abandoned, half eaten. The air thickened with unspoken desires and grew heavy with silence. Everyone seemed, out of politeness, or politics, to be holding their breath, unwilling to be the first to speak. Only Emma, whose anxiety far outweighed polite forbearance, said quickly, 'I want to be with Mama!'

To her surprise, and her sisters' annoyance, none of the adults disagreed – except perhaps Mrs Rount, who was not used to spoilt girls, and who raised her eyebrows and turned down the corners of her mouth with disgust, becoming vociferous in the discussion that followed. Like animated playing-cards, the little group shuffled and dealt themselves into two hands, discovered that those hands were not perfect, reshuffled and dealt again, offering opinions to each other all the while.

Her own objective accomplished, Emma sat on the grass,

pulling out daisy-heads and watching the others. She became aware that in all the talk, Mama and Mr Steer were the only ones who said nothing: they did not speak and they did not look at each other. This should have made Emma pleased, but it struck her instead as something she could not find a reason for. It became another unanswerable question, and her apprehensiveness returned. She spied on them from beneath lowered eyelashes and saw how they held themselves back, as though what they wanted, what they secretly wished, was too precious ever to be spoken. It did not occur to Emma that, unlike her, they could not properly voice their simple request to sit side by side in the chaise. Instead Philip stared at a blade of grass that he drew repeatedly through his fingers as though trying to memorise its greenness and the way the fine ribs on it caught the sunlight as he pulled it. Emma hoped it would cut him. She turned her attention to her mother. Isobel lay back in her rattan chair as though she had no interest in the discussions at all. She was swinging a fringe at the end of the sash of her dress slowly to and fro, as if completely abandoned to the momentum of fate. She looked up briefly, her calm features composed into such blankness that they startled Emma, and seeing her daughter's stare smiled weakly, as though it cost her great effort, from somewhere far away.

Dunwich lay four miles along the coast from Walberswick, where the marsh ended and the ground rose steeply to a hill that ran straight out into the sea. No more than a hamlet, it lay strung out along a country lane that ended suddenly on a wide, white beach, running into shingle near the lifeboat house and the tarred fishermen's huts in the lee of the cliff. You could find the fishermen there in the late afternoon, knotting their nets and watching the gulls wheel above the tiny church of All Saints, perched on the very edge of the promontory; while the sea sucked at the cliff-base and year by year more of the foundations of the church clattered into the waves. They would talk of how the land fought a ceaseless, speechless battle with the sea, and shake their heads. It wasn't just the crumbling of the cliff or the licking tongues of waves that crept a little further up the beach every day, or the way the sea rushed on wild nights up the main street of the village to plunder what it could.

Dunwich had once been the capital of the kingdom of East Anglia, a city that now lay far below the tide-line, all its palaces and churches gloated over by the waves. You could still feel its presence, said the fishermen, if you stood on the beach very early in the morning before the dawn had quite gone, or in the evening as the light faded and the darkness came in silently over the sea. A mysterious, magnetic feeling. And some of them claimed that when a storm raged they could hear the wild clanging of church bells through the howling of the wind and the pounding of the water.

The Romans, finding safe harbour in the lee of the cliff and a good look-out place to guard their new-found province from attack by sea, called it Sitomagus. The Angles made it a centre for commerce. Long, long after the Angles, the Knights Templar came. They built a preceptory and adjoining houses and lived in elegant piety with all the luxury the Middle Ages could afford. And long after them, to save the soul of the community from the memory of such heresy, the Franciscans came and built a great monastery, constructing it, like wise Christians, not on the sinking sands which had slid so many souls into the sea, but high on the crown of the hill, with a flint wall around the highest contour of the hill, to protect it.

It was this wall, looping white like a banner among the blackthorn and may trees, that Emma first saw as they came to the crossroads in the middle of the village, their chaise pausing for a moment before veering right up the hill. The village, as they passed through, seemed deserted and quiet in the heat of the summer's afternoon, and Emma, sunk drowsily against her mother's shoulder, thought that there was, perhaps, no fête after all. But even as the horses' hooves fell momentarily silent, there was a great shout from somewhere above them, rhythmic clapping broke out, and the squeak and thump of a band could be heard, gaining strength and cohesion. The horses surged forward, swaying into the steep slope, in and out of patches of deep shade and bright sunlight, and Emma, clutching her mother's arm with one hand and her hat with the other, looked up and saw a great plume of smoke suddenly curl up above the crown of the hill. They turned a bend in the road, and beside them the wall emerged from a thicket of elder and soared up, high as a church. Their ponies slowed to a walk. The verges were crammed with carts and tethered horses: patient shires beribboned and bejewelled with brasses, their hooves oiled, their plaited tails ceaselessly whisking away flies, their ears twitching and their noses half in a bag of oats. There were farmers' gigs of varnished wood, each with a pony tethered a safe distance away, asleep on its feet. Under some of the vehicles dogs were tied, stretched out dozing. A couple looked up as the two chaises went past; one of them growled and the other bared its teeth silently. Surly looking men leaned in ones and twos against the wall, horseminders, with small eyes and swarthy brown arms, their shirt-sleeves rolled up to the elbow. They looked with curiosity and distaste at the newcomers and one of them spat into the roadway.

The chaises came to an uneasy standstill, but for a moment no one seemed very willing to descend. It was the Reverend Rount who jumped down first, beaming fiercely at everyone. Then Emma was swung down and stood on the road staring through the delicately fluted stone arch, which was all that remained of the gate to the Franciscan monastery. Someone took her hand and they walked forward. The music gathered its strength and swept them up as a great crowd of people swirled towards them over the bumpy grass. Laughed and jostled and swayed close. Red faces and wide-open mouths, arms linked together like a string of fat sausages, huge boots and dirty, crooked toes. A wall of sweat and worsted and stale beer that suddenly danced away from them, and was replaced by a thin waft of blue smoke which blew across their path, stinging their eyes and smelling of burnt fat and hot flesh. The band stopped and the chain of dancers fragmented into twos and threes, still whirling slowly like leaves released from a gust of wind. Children ran out among them as though to catch the last breath of sound, jigging up and down, clapping their hands and then running self-consciously back into the crowd.

The party made their way across the grass to where their hosts waited on a line of chairs. Emma, her hand still tightly held, was the first to reach them and was pushed forward to do her curtsies – the doctor's wife, the Colonel's wife, the Colonel's unmarried daughter – while before her, behind her, all around her, the crowd stared and Emma stumbled in the tufts of grass, blushing at the ignominy of being made part of the entertainment.

Her ordeal over, she turned to look for her mother. Isobel had been swallowed up in the general process of introductions; the Colonel, much taken by her, had her gloved fingers firmly pressed between his own large hands and seemed to have forgotten to let go. He was talking to Philip, who stood nervously close to Isobel as though afraid they might be separated. Mrs Rount was pushing her way forward to ingratiate herself with the Colonel's wife, and Aunt Jude and Mrs Morris, chatting as though old friends, had already found themselves chairs.

Aunt Jude looked up and saw Emma's worried gaze. 'Come and sit down, dear,' she said, and patted the seat next to her.

Emma shook her head. The band started up again, and the party hastened to settle themselves. Emma scrambled towards her mother, reaching her just as Isobel and Philip, smiling quickly into each other's eyes at the good fortune of finding chairs together, were sitting down. She pushed between them.

'Emma!'

Emma threw herself on to the chair that was to have been Philip's, holding on tightly, as though she expected to be dragged off it. She looked beseechingly at her mother and then turned to glare at Philip, who stared stonily back at her. The only spare chair was at the far end of the line, next to the Colonel's unmarried daughter. He had, by the engineering of Mrs Rount, been prevented from driving to Dunwich in the same chaise as Isobel; now it seemed his prize was to be taken from under his nose again.

Isobel put an arm round Emma, drawing her towards her. 'You're disrupting everything, darling, squeeze on the edge of my chair.'

From the coveted position of Isobel's side, encircled by her arm, Emma leaned against her mother's bosom and watched Mr Steer settle himself stiffly beside them. She saw him glance over her head at her mother with fleetingly injured eyes, but her mother was engaged in adjusting the brim of her hat against the afternoon sun. Emma alone saw his expression, calculated the effect of her mischief, felt a warm glow of malicious pleasure, and then forgot about him completely as she gave all her attention to the dancing that had begun again.

A piccolo soared like a small bird, so high you felt you could hardly hear it any more, until it spiralled down to flutter about your head; below it a drum thumped, earthbound and mindless; cymbals crashed erratically; and through it all thudded the dancers' feet as they jumped backwards and forwards, running slow and heavy under arches of hands. Isobel turned to Philip, her eyes shining.

'"The Sprig o' May!"' she whispered excitedly.

'What is it?' Philip bent across Emma as though she weren't there.

'"The Sprig o' May". They used to dance it in our village when I was a little girl.' She turned her head again to watch the dancers. The movements were familiar and yet she could not quite anticipate them. The shape of the dance and the refrain of the song prodded dormant images in her brain until the words fell into place and the faces of the dancers became overlaid with other faces. Faces from her youth: servants from her father's house, farmhands, village people. Faces that had bent over her all her childhood, large and gentle, with the quiet deference of country people, suddenly seen on occasions such as these outside the context of the servants' stairs and the acres of folding sheets. Above bright dresses and amid a swirl of scarves and fluttering ribbons, the faces were flushed and shining with a purpose never before seen in them, dark with an intent that grasped Isobel by the throat, until she felt she could not breathe without knowing what it was. And none of them would stop to tell her; they were all too far away in another world, linking arms, turning and turning under the lime trees beside the cricket pitch while the twilight of those long, summer evenings crept on leaf by leaf, the boldness of the dancers increasing as the darkness came. Isobel could see her parents sitting stiffly on chairs that had been put out for them, growing paler in the deepening blue, as though all their power were being drawn out of them, leaving only insubstantial shadows. The dancers changed too, until they were no longer Molly and Tom and Nell from the servants' hall, but fierce, bright creatures. Dancing, Isobel had thought from the timidity of her childhood, does this to people. Makes them wild and bright and strong. And she had longed for the years to pass until she too could go to dances. But it had never happened the way she thought it would. In those hot, glittering ballrooms, she felt only anxiety: it was all new dresses and pounding hearts. And the music was so different. She had forgotten about her dreams of release. Until this afternoon, hearing the music again.

Philip stared greedily at Isobel, oblivious to the impropriety of his stare. He fed upon the raptness of her expression, the profile of her face as it bent in eagerness towards the dancers, and longed to have her whole attention for himself. He tried to imagine how their life might be together. Would she gaze with such raptness at the dancers in the music-halls, where he and Sickert went in the evenings to sketch? He thought of the walks across London, through the wet November darkness, how there would be the warmth of the woman beside him, the pressure of her hand on his arm, the catch of her breath in the frosty air – and the look of amazement on Walter's face: 'This is Isobel, old man . . . ' But it wouldn't do. At that point the dream slipped out of perspective, like a painting that goes suddenly wrong. The image of the darkness faded, and the smell of the frost-wet streets. Sunshine took over, harshly bright, intolerant of illusion: the tinny squeak and thump of the band grated on his ears and the garish figures jumped up and down in a parody of romance. And his longing was sharpened by the impossibility of it all.

At the end of the row of chairs, Mrs Rount leaned forward from what she considered the ignominy of her position. As she did so, the dancers gave their final bow. Amidst the sporadic clapping and cat-calls she could see the Colonel laughing and shouting out, 'Bravo!' Beside him her husband, beaming and red-faced, was clapping loudly as though he had enjoyed the whole thing hugely. Mrs Rount drew in her neck and sat back against her hard chair. 'Well he might,' she thought sourly, 'sitting where *he* is!'

Philip found the tableaux-vivants that followed dreary to the point of boredom. Schoolchildren draped in white sheets and cast-off curtains skipped over the grass in an interminable game of 'statues', freezing suddenly into groups of unfathomable regal or colonial significance. In his cast-down mood, he found himself glancing often towards Isobel, as though to find some cause for hope in the profile of her face. From time to time

Isobel would seem to feel his gaze on her and would turn her head to him with varying expressions of indulgent amusement at the antics of the children in front of her. As Philip watched, her sideways looks became increasingly more frequent until each time he turned to her he found her, in that instant, turning to him. It was like some secret magic, some extra dimension of communication that had suddenly been revealed to them. It became, for them, more exciting than kisses. Utterly caught up in their own game, they believed that all other eyes must be on the children. Isobel had lost sight of the skipping figures in front of her; the expression in her eyes was no longer one of maternal indulgence. She had taken on a dazed, almost blinded, stare that Philip drank in. Their bodies sat stiffly side by side while their minds raced together, and when finally a shadow fell across them, it was only the involuntary blinking of their eyes that brought them back to consciousness and the dangers of their situation. For the Colonel, standing directly in front of them, was about to begin his Address to the Queen.

Emma hardly heard the Colonel's speech; words like 'glory' and 'allegiance' floated above her head. She stared at the motion-less tableau-vivant with envy and longed to take part herself. To dance in a white sheet with a silver ribbon round her head in front of all these people. She gazed at the diminutive figure in its red velveteen curtain. To have been chosen for the part of Queen Empress! To have been drawn on to the field on a sled decorated with tinsel, wearing a gold-coloured crown and having pink paper flowers thrown in one's way – to be queen for an hour!

Suddenly a raucous cheer went up from the far side of the field and around her a forest of dark-suited legs and swirling skirts rose to the sound. From their midst, Emma could see nothing. She craned her neck back, but all she could see was sky. She looked down again, and there were everybody's boots trampling the grass, so she looked at her hands as Miss Brand had taught her and wondered what Queen Victoria was doing at that precise moment.

In fact, the event that was claiming everyone's attention was the arrival of the Jubilee Supper. Trestle tables had been laid out in a large square, and the ox, which had been roasting all day, was being carved up on a smaller table close by. There was now a general rush towards these tables, a rush of eager expectation that surged forward in a wave of children and drink-hungry men and then was drawn back again on a tide of deference. Into this lull stepped the Colonel's party and made their way to the top table, where the men settled the ladies into their chairs with as much gallantry as if they were in the dining room at the Hall. Behind them the villagers jostled and squabbled for places around the other three tables. When all were settled the Reverend Rount banged on the table in front of him for silence. First he blessed the Queen, under whose guidance the country had accrued such wealth and glory; then he blessed the bounty of the Colonel, from whose farms the ox had been given; and then he bade them all thank God for their good fortune. Wooden platters were passed eagerly from hand to hand, ale was poured from large earthenware jugs, and in the first silent frenzy of eating (for this was the first meat most of the villagers had tasted since Christmas), the nicety of their betters at the top table was forgotten. Healths to Her Majesty followed each other so fast they soon became Healths Incoherent. Greasy fingers slid surreptitiously round neighbouring waists, children squabbled for bones and the old men nodded at each other in a satiated stupor and agreed that perhaps theirs was the best of all possible lives under the best of all possible rulers after all.

The band struck up again to wild thumping on the tables and raucous shouts of approval of this new diversion. Several of the villagers swayed to their feet to dance. Emma and Philip, side by side, stared mournfully down at them from the top table. Emma, bolstered on sacks which someone had rolled into a discarded cloak, deliberately stared out over the crowd in order to ignore Philip. Philip had been seated next to her mother instead of her, but he didn't seem to benefit much from it for Mama was always turned away from him towards the Colonel. She saw how the Colonel's monopoly of Isobel crushed Philip, how he stared at the back of Isobel's head and looked up hopefully when she turned again to her plate. Emma heard the beginnings of sentences with which he tried to capture her attention and which died in mid-syllable as the Colonel's voice, rising again, drowned them out.

Now the crowded, feasting tables in front of her were emptying. Small groups of people huddled together on the benches round remnants of ale jugs, their arms over each other's shoulders, heads bowed together, then suddenly flying apart in a shriek of laughter and crowding in again, mouths wide open for the next tale. Others sat quietly as though contentedly full, beating time to the band on the greasy surface of their table with mugs or clean-picked bones, crooning and swaying to themselves. Over where the tableaux had been, they were dancing, whooping and screaming with delight as one couple crashed into another, or tripped on a tussock of grass. Dogs gnawed at bones clasped protectively between their paws, growling softly at anyone who stepped too near. In and out of the ruins children darted, like bats, shrieking. The light of early evening darkened, and as the blueness deepened the warmth seemed to drain out of the air. Emma's sacking cushion had lost its buoyancy, and the meat on her plate had become cold and greasy. Over her head, the doctor's wife struck up a conversation with Philip. Emma, ignored, felt herself sinking beneath the surface of the table so low that she seemed no longer to be present at the feast at all. The grown-ups had taken over again, suddenly, without warning. She looked to the left of her at the ornate silver buckle of the doctor's wife's dress, and then to the right of her. Mama's dress seemed to spill out over Philip's chair. She screwed up her eyes and looked harder – there seemed to be no space at all between Mama's back and Philip's side. There was no space: the harder she stared the more clearly she could see the shadow where their bodies met. Philip had not been sitting in misery all through supper, he had been leaning against Mama. It was warm and nice to lean against Mama, that was what she had wanted to do. Rage boiled up inside her, but before she could pull Philip away from Isobel, everyone around her, as though at a signal, pushed back their chairs.

The Colonel began to hand round cigars. Isobel turned to smile at Philip and then pushed her chair back too, so that without his having to move at all he became part of the Colonel's group. But he refused a cheroot, shaking his head and smiling silently. The old man leaned back in his chair to light his own.

'Good for the midges.' He winked at Isobel. 'Come on, young Steer, you're not smoking. Why not take Mrs Heatherington out on to the dance floor? Someone should show willing and join in. We old fogies can't go jigging about on that field. You young 'uns run along and do duty for us.'

The thought of the pleasure of dancing with Isobel overwhelmed Philip and he rose to his feet with a solemnity that made one think he moved only under extreme duress. He hardly dared look at Isobel, but stood in front of her with downcast eyes. Her face as serious as his, she rose, laying one hand on his arm, and they walked quickly away from the group at the table without speaking further or even looking at each other.

Philip led her through the crowds towards the far side of the dance floor. She felt the unevenness of the field through her thin shoes and wondered if she would stumble. She saw the swallows dive and Philip bow politely as he halted in front of her. She put her hand on his shoulder and felt his arm go round her waist. There they stood, looking solemnly at each other, ready to begin, but unsure quite how to, like two children at a dancing lesson. Around them thudded the music. The young blades of the village whirled their partners past in a flurry of skirts and breathless shrieks. The older couples jigged sedately round and round. One fellow leaned towards Isobel as he thundered level with her and smiled broadly. 'You'd best start, ma'am, you'm safer movin' 'n standin' still – we shouldn't want to knock 'ee down.' And he was gone.

'I think,' began Philip, 'a sort of waltz?'

He wished suddenly that he had been to more dances; it was terrible to have Isobel in his arms and to be so inept. But it wasn't a waltz.

'A polka?' suggested Isobel, shouting against the music.

'Ah!' said Philip, frowning with the effort of changing step in mid-stream.

They found themselves eddied into the quieter centre of the grassy patch while the current of dancers whirled on round the circumference. Here in this calm they felt protected from the curious stares of the villagers, the couples who twirled and flashed about them screening them from prying eyes. They almost felt cut off from the need to dance at all, and stood happily smiling at each other as though they were at last alone in some quiet place. It was quite without their help that their feet began to find a small jigging step that satisfied the rhythm of the band and fulfilled the conventions of the dance, so that the position of their arms round each other's bodies was justified, and gradually the interest of the other dancers in this strangely static couple waned. The band obligingly played from one tune into another with scarcely a pause. All that Philip and Isobel were aware of was the swaying of their bodies together; the unaccustomed, long-awaited closeness of the other; the smell of their skin . . . the scent of their hair . . . the light pressure of their hands . . .

Chapter Ten

Shortly before dawn Philip fell asleep. When he woke again it was to a harsh, white light that seeped in behind the curtains to flood the room. He woke suddenly in a terror of having overslept and in the ragged numbness of hardly having slept at all. Echoes of a song reverberated in his head, the room seemed to whirl slowly around him as if it, or he, were still dancing, and his arms felt warm as though Isobel had only just left them. Alarmed by the intimacy of these sensations he leapt out of bed: to compromise Isobel, of all people, with such thoughts! He stood quite still – what if he had compromised Isobel already, last night, in front of all those people? He stumbled, dry-mouthed and blinking, over to the bell-pull, and when the girl came snapped at her that he wanted breakfast in his room. When she'd gone he slumped back on to the bed, fumbling over the things on the night table to find his watch, struggling with stiff fingers to open the silver lid. Then he sat staring at the engraved face, watching the hand move millimetre by millimetre, watching the shadow fall across the hour, clear it and move on over the white enamel surface. He stared fixedly, as though trying to petrify its movement, feeling himself powerless and stupid in front of the immutability of time. He might smash the watch, tear out its filigree hands, but he was still trapped. Time pounded silently and rhythmically in the air all around him; it shook at the fabric of his life like the reverberation of cannon in an unseen war. His life past, his life present, even his life to come – it was marked out in seconds, already, one by one.

He struggled to his feet and began to gather his clothes together, making short runs between the chest of drawers and the bed with a strange tiptoeing gait, piling everything up on the bed. The serving girl came in with his breakfast tray and he motioned her towards the table near the window. She stared at him open-mouthed, and went hurriedly downstairs again to tell Mrs Pearce that the gentleman from London had been took queer and was running round his room in his nightshirt, and the drawers in the chest all pulled out and his things all strewn everywhere.

When Mrs Pearce knocked at the door of his room, she found him on his knees, searching under the bed for his bags.

'Lord save us, Mr Steer,' she exclaimed, 'you're not leaving us!'

'Ah!' Philip, surprised, leapt up, and as he did so the catch on the Gladstone bag he was holding sprang itself and the lid flew open, as though in a conjuring trick. Startled, they both peered inside at its empty cavernousness.

'I am expected . . . ' burst out Philip, clutching the bag shut as though it had committed an impropriety.

Mrs Pearce's eyes widened.

' . . . in France!'

And her mouth dropped open.

Having given himself such firm direction, he dressed and packed and ate his breakfast with such speed that his hands shook. But all the while he felt a sinking dread at what he had done. In a moment, with just a few words, he had pushed himself on to another track altogether, so that now he was preparing to depart when all he wanted to do was stay.

He sat in the empty room, staring about him mournfully to make sure there was no forgotten tube of paint or necktie lurking. He should, he thought, write notes of farewell. But he had packed his writing materials. He rang for the servant girl, but it was Mrs Pearce who appeared. She came no farther than the doorway and stood with folded arms, a glint of piqued rage in her eyes as she spied the bags, ready strapped, at his feet.

'There's no train,' she snapped, 'till two. So I took the liberty of ordering the carter to be here twelve-thirty sharp. Will you want lunch before you go?' She spoke as if she intended to dish up hemlock.

'No, thank you.' He could not bring himself to ask her for paper and ink. 'If you would prepare my bill. I . . . I hope to see you again before the summer is out . . . if my business in France is accomplished within the month. I do most certainly hope to come back . . . '

If Mrs Pearce had made him feel she disbelieved every word of excuse he made for his sudden departure, convincing Smytheson was even worse. He stood on the terrace by the old man's chair, wringing his hands and talking of promises to join artist friends in Étaples for the month of July and an unexpected summons to business in London that necessitated immediate departure.

'Well, this is sudden, Philip,' was all the old man said, but his questioning look as Philip's story got more and more entangled suggested that nothing was lost on him.

'Perhaps,' ventured Philip, as he shook Smytheson's hand, 'you would say, you would offer – regrets – to Mrs Heatherington and her aunt for me?' He smiled weakly and tried to disengage his hand, but the old man held on to it.

'Ah,' he said sympathetically, 'because time is so short?'

'Exactly,' breathed Philip.

'Off with you!' Smytheson threw up Philip's hand as though releasing a falcon into the air. 'Bow farewell to Mrs Heatherington, kiss her aunt's hand and rush out again!'

Philip had no choice but to leave after that. The old man had judged and now sat smiling, calm and Buddha-like in the sunshine, his hands clasped contentedly across his stomach, his eyelids half closed against the glare.

'Well then, adieu,' said Philip awkwardly.

The old man nodded and his eyelids flickered, like a lizard.

Philip walked away across the buzzing, sunlit garden, in and out of the great pools of shadow cast by the huge, forbidding yews. Out on the road it was all whiteness and dust, and the choking heat of midday. He came opposite 'The Anchor' and felt himself trembling, hot trickles of perspiration running down inside his shirt and beading along his forehead under the band of his hat. If the carter had been standing in the inn yard he would have grasped at the chance to leave immediately, but he was not.

As he made the descent towards the harbour, he saw Emma and her sisters straggling up the road from the beach. They met at the gate of Quay House and Philip was thrown into further confusion by the bobbing curtsies, the blushing, the bowing which got awkwardly mixed up with his attempts to open the little wrought-iron gate into the garden for them, and Emma's persistent, frowning enquiries about whether he had come for lunch. When they had all three filed past him, he took a deep breath and announced to their backs that he had called in, very briefly, to say farewell on his way to France. Simultaneously, they paused in their journey down the garden path, turned their heads, and stared at him with what he later recalled as maliciously pleased eyes. He was even more disconcerted by the fact that they said nothing – not even that they were sorry he was going – and that, on reaching the front door, they burst helter-skelter through it, leaving him to the ministrations of the maid, who was so loaded down with buckets, spades, shrimping-nets and plaid rugs that she could not even take his hat.

He stood in the hall by himself and thought what a mess he had made of everything. How much better he might have managed things if he had waited a few days, announcing his departure before he took it, instead of rushing off in a blind panic like this. Sickert was not leaving for Étaples until the first of July; there would have been time . . . He heard a rustle on the stairs, followed by a clattering, and looking up saw Isobel surrounded by her children. He took in first the sisters' hard, impassive faces, the faces of messengers who have delivered, with concealed pleasure, disagreeable news; then his eyes moved quickly to Isobel's face, and read instantly the effect of that message. She came towards him, her daughters clustering close behind her with the eagerness of hound puppies curious to witness a kill. The only sound was the snuffling, shuffling noise of long skirts as the women moved. It ground into his senses like minute fragments of shattered glass that were to lie sharp in his memory for years to come. The pain of it made him bound forward, one hand held out to her.

'I am sorry . . . ' he began.

But she kept her hands loosely folded against her waist and went on regarding him with an unbearable expression of hurt disbelief. Her voice, when it came, was decorously calm. 'I hear you are leaving us.'

With an instinct of self-preservation that Philip was later to deplore to Sickert as the most dishonourable cowardice, he took advantage of her silent reserve to become voluble. 'I had, as you know, engaged myself to join friends in France for the month of July – an annual sketching trip, that we have fallen into the habit of taking, to Étaples. Étaples, do you know it? Just across the channel. A place very like Walberswick.'

He realised he was running on, rambling, tripping himself up, falling further in her estimation. 'I shall think of you all often, there,' he added plaintively.

But the expressions on their faces did not alter.

'I do hope to return after it is over . . . and regret very much that I have to leave so suddenly, but some business of my mother's which has dragged on and must be concluded before I leave the country necessitates . . . '

There was an uncomfortable silence in which he remembered with concern that the carter must now be waiting in the inn yard for him.

'Will you give my sincerest regards to your aunt?'

At last she held out her hand to him and he felt once again the softness of her skin. He bent his head briefly over it and its delicate perfume enveloped him. He looked up into her eyes before he turned away, and remembered how they had danced in each other's arms all night long.

Throughout the journey to London, Philip sat pressed against the window of the railway carriage, staring not at the country-side beyond but at his own reflection in the glass. His lips moved continuously, and from time to time his hands, resting on his knees, would clench themselves. 'If only,' he said to himself over and over again, 'if only I could have seen Isobel alone.' If only he could have been honest. If only he could have told her how the realisation that their passion was mutual had so terrified him that his only thought was of the enormity of the sin they might commit, and how, in his miserable inade-quacy, his first thought had been of flight when all he really wanted was to be with her. How he was, he knew, doing the right thing, but in the wrong way. He shook his head sadly to himself. His only consolation was that if he couldn't tell Isobel, at least he could tell Sickert. He would call on him first thing on his way back to Addison Road from the station; he would invite him to dine that very evening. Sickert would know what to do – he fell in love half a dozen times a month. He would tell Sickert everything.

'Why Steer, old man, come in, come in! Don't hover in the hall, come upstairs to the studio.'

'Well, no,' replied Philip, 'I can't. I've got a cab waiting outside.'

He stood on the doormat looking anxiously up at his friend. Walter Sickert was perched on the lowest step of the staircase, paintbrush in hand. From this vantage point he could see that all was not well with Philip. Even discounting the livid greens and purples that shone on him from the coloured glass of the fanlight, he looked paler than ever, formal and listless in his travelling clothes. His eyes were those of a retriever who despairs of ever finding quarry again.

'I came,' said Philip, twisting his fingers together, 'to ask you whether you would dine with me tonight . . . '

'I'd be delighted! Now where – ?'

' . . . and I wondered – you remember our trip to Étaples – I wondered whether I might join you in France after all?'

'But you wrote,' Sickert grinned and pointed his paintbrush at Philip. 'You wrote from your precious Walberswick retreat to say that things were going so well among the birds and the flowers that you'd changed your mind about Étaples.'

'I know.'

'I suspect,' went on Walter, 'that you've been warbling after feathers on hats, rather than feathers on wings. I shall expect to hear all this evening.'

'You shall.' Philip felt a spreading glow of relief. 'You shall. I'll pick you up at six.'

'Bring your sketchbook with you,' shouted Walter as Philip closed the door behind him, 'and we'll go on after to Gatti's.'

Philip's rooms, like all uninhabited houses, had died a little during his absence, had withdrawn and puckered into desiccation, allowing themselves to be smothered by the fine dust of a London summer, as though it were earth. There were dead flies along the windowsills, and against one windowpane in the studio a mummified Red Admiral pressed in supplication against the glass. Philip sank on to the day bed, pushing aside the bundles of old curtaining that he sometimes used for drapery in his portraits. He took off his jacket and lay back among the cushions, pulling at his tie and then unhooking his collar stud to open his shirt. He had an hour before he had to go out to dinner. He closed his eyes.

The sound of train wheels still racketed in his head. Like the images of a bioscope, fields and hedges bounded past the train windows, the fast sweep of a green valley, the flickering of woods, the parched streak of a hayfield and the turgid glide of acres of corn passed in his head, slowing as he drifted into sleep, and stopping, as the boundary into the unconscious was crossed, on an image of a level crossing. Through the bars of the crossing-gates, Philip could see the white dust of a gravelled road, a pair of cottages huddled by the signal-box, a horse that pranced, ears laid back, away from the shrieking train, the upturned face of a man laughing, who leaned against the gate, one arm thrown negligently across the topmost bar as if caressingly protecting both the gleaming metal animal that raced along its tracks and the frightened horse that danced behind him on the road.

It was a picture that flickered for a moment in his mind before the images began moving again, erratically, faster and faster, tumbling one after the other in the illusion of great speed, so that it took him a little time to realise that now they were moving backwards. Hills suddenly crashed down into valleys, and woods rose up again; a station flashed by and a whirlwind of people were sucked on to the train or expelled from it with such lightning speed that even in his dream Philip felt a fleeting concern that someone might be injured. Instead of the suburbs of London crawling out to meet them, the train hurtled backwards into ever more desolate countryside. A thin sliver of water shone like a beckoning finger among reeds, broadening quickly into a river, then into an estuary, creeked and mud-flatted, traced out by skeins of mournful birds. But before the railway could reach the sea, Philip found himself standing on what seemed to be a vast moorland, alone, the train having vanished as silently as if it had never been.

Night had fallen with unexplained suddenness. He stood in the darkness and felt heather pricking through his socks and bracken fronds pressing up against his legs. Around him, low bushes crouched in strange attitudes; to his left, he could feel the massive body of the sea breathing rhythmically in the night. He could smell its saltiness, the resin of the pines that stood in battered clumps about the heath and a cool sweetness coming from the moor itself, that one never smelt by day. And then he realised where he was.

He began to walk forward with a feeling of surprise and elation at discovering himself to be exactly where he wanted to be. Presently, the heath gave way to turf and the sea spread out before him, the night seeming to lighten as his eyes accustomed themselves to the darkness. The sheeptrack he was on divided and divided again. To his right, a line of dark trees rose up. He made towards them, for that was where the village lay. Only one house was visible, standing between Philip and the sea, protected from the common by a high black wall. As he neared the trees a figure detached itself from the darkness and swung forward to meet him, arms outstretched, the face shadowed black by the moon. Philip felt his own hands reach out, felt almost within his grasp the fulfilment of all his desires. Then, suddenly, a suffocation seemed to strangle him. He threw back his head, gasping for breath, but none came. His chest would not move. His hands scrabbled at the air to clasp those other hands held out to him, his feet pounded against the ground to cross the minute distance that finally separated them. But nothing moved — not the earth, not the trees — only the two humans, flailing helplessly in their longing.

The dream accompanied Philip to France and visited him almost every night, leaving him tired and dispirited every morning. It never varied, and it ended always at this point: On the days following the rare nights it did not come, Philip felt lost and anxious, unable to settle to any work, and waited only for the day to be over and night to fall, so that the longed-for torment could begin again.

Chapter Eleven

The weather that July was held to be extraordinarily fine. From the last week of June the sun had set itself into a rare pattern of clear, blue days, and the whole of England basked in unaccustomed heat. Even St Swithun's Day passed without a cloud in the sky. The heatwave established itself in general conversation as a phenomenon. Someone coined the phrase 'Queen's Weather' and it caught the imagination of a nation still ebullient from the celebration of Victoria's Jubilee. The country glowed with self-satisfaction, unaware or else dismissive of the corrosion of their Empire overseas or of the liberalisation of the social and moral structures of life at home, which would sweep away the rigid foundations on which their complacency rested. News travelled slowly in the provinces and consisted mainly of the state of the harvest or the price of a pig at market. The illusion that life could continue as it always had was regarded as a certainty, and in the self-absorbed depths of Suffolk, agricultural reforms seemed as distant as the colonies beyond the Indian Ocean that dared to fight for independence from the Empire.

In the fields around Walberswick, grass was being cut for hay, tendrils of barley began to stiffen, oats to bleach and wheat to fatten. Morning and evening the local farmers rode their boundaries, pulling at the green ears of corn as they passed, rolling the grains that came loose between their fingers with a far-away look in their eyes as they calculated the harvests to come and squinted at the sky to gauge the next day's weather. The fishermen kept watch not only on the sky, but also on the sea. They stared at its calm surface day after day with distrust, as at the unaccustomed affability of a quick-tempered woman. They went out fishing at night, when it was cooler, and frequently were becalmed, floating in on the morning tide with empty nets and empty bellies. Some of the young ones gave up in disgust and went off with the day labourers to try their luck hay-making, stone-picking, bird-scaring, or harvesting.

Joining the straggling groups of men, women and children in the lanes and field paths that led away from the village, who stumbled half asleep, shivering with cold in those grey dawns before the sun came up or any animal stirred, making for their appointed work places.

Emma and her sisters spent every day on the beach now, in the care of one or other of the maids. Their initial inhibitions about public beach life had quite disappeared and they had entered the proprietorial phase common to summer visitors. They strutted up and down the sand, or probed in the shallows at the water's edge, calling to each other in voices that spiralled up to reverberate against the blue dome of the sky: the curious echo of summer, which we remember all our lives.

Aunt Jude, too, spent almost every day out of doors: the sun reanimated her and she basked in it, shimmering and sparkling. A familiar, bulky figure in a large straw hat, she could be seen most afternoons either visiting in the village or sitting with her grand-nieces on the beach. Her mornings, however, were spent with Mr Smytheson on the terrace of Quay House. They had, without quite planning it, established a ritual which became the focus of their day. Just before eleven every morning, Mr Smytheson could be observed leaving the shaded sanctuary of his garden and emerging on to the dusty village street, looking as dapper as if he were taking a stroll in Hyde Park. 'Doctor's orders', he called his morning constitutional, or, with a wink, 'remedial exercise'. Whether it was the restorative effect of Aunt Jude's good-humoured company, or of the sun, his step became firmer as the summer wore on. He would round the terrace of Quay House, panting slightly from his exertions, and stand there beaming at his friend as she sat ensconced in a wicker chair.

'How are the bones?' Aunt Jude would ask, putting down her embroidery.

For answer he would draw himself up, stand very straight before her and rap sharply on the flagstones with his cane, like a sergeant-major demanding order. 'Improvin' ma'am, improvin' every day!'

He would draw up a chair next to her, lower himself stiffly into it and recount the news from that morning's *Times*. She would then tell of the latest cleverness of her great-nieces, and from there they would proceed to discuss the world in general or Walberswick in particular. Sometimes they would be joined by Isobel, who would float out from the open French windows behind them to subside in ruffled layers of muslin on to a chaise-longue. She would interrupt their calm conversation with a trail of frivolities, fanning herself with a large hat, simpering at Mr Smytheson across its brim, insisting that he stay to lunch and constantly engaging her aunt as corroborative witness to everything she said in a tiresomely affected way. They would both be relieved when, running out of chatter, Isobel would leave with the excuse that she had to tell Cook there would be a guest to lunch.

She would indeed put her head in at the kitchen door, but her real objective was to seek the sanctuary of the hot, deserted house. She would run upstairs on tiptoe, pausing on the landing to make sure all was silent, and pace from room to room, greedily drinking in the solitude. It was as though each time she flung open a door on an empty room, she gained some temporary relief. Sometimes she would lean against one of the walls for minutes at a time, her face pressed against it, her arms outstretched along its length, her mind floating, lost and aimless. Then, with a start, she would recollect herself and set off again, prowling the empty corridors, a certain impatience in her step as though she sought something she could not find, or awaited the arrival of something unaccountably delayed. She would trail her fingers across the windowpanes, making the trapped flies buzz. And, feeling her eyes fill with tears, she would shake her head, as if unable to believe what was happening to her, whispering to herself in a cracked, dry, puzzled voice, 'I cannot bear it, I cannot bear it . . . '

It was the heat, she told herself. It was this terrible, relentless heat that made her so restless. It was the way her clothes pressed against her so tightly that made sitting down unbearable and standing so pointless. Nothing, it seemed to her, would ever have point again. How people could indulge in such indolent gaiety in the face of such heat was beyond her comprehension. She wanted only to be alone. But no sooner had she gained the solitude she sought than guilt would begin to gnaw at her, and its alarming presence, hinting at other guilts, drove her down to Aunt Jude again. There she would sit at her aunt's side, staring out at the brilliant garden without even seeing it, full of an unassuaged feeling of confusion and incompleteness. Aunt Jude at such times learned to leave her alone.

'She suffers so, you know, in this heat,' she would confide to Mr Smytheson. But she privately sought some other explanation for her niece's distraction. Sometimes Isobel caught her aunt staring at her with puzzled concern, staring as one might at an inanimate object, closely and without restraint. Those glances told her more about herself than her looking-glass could. They alarmed her into admitting that she was being noticed, that her complaints about the heat had become too numerous to be convincing. She knew it was something more than sunshine that drained the life out of her, and she began to fear that others might speculate on just what else it might be. So she would turn to her aunt and smile wanly into that penetrating gaze, rolling her damp handkerchief nervously between the palms of her hands, and say, 'I do wish it would rain,' in a voice perilously near to tears.

In the evening, Isobel would wander sometimes round the garden after dinner, while the children were being put to bed. But even the approaching coolness of night offered little comfort. The heat still hung in the garden as though in an enclosed room. It was the time when roses and honeysuckle smelled their sweetest, an enveloping, sharp sweetness that made Isobel despair of ever achieving peace of mind again. When, after their evening watering, the leaves dripped on to soil that hissed and sucked noisily at the moisture releasing a scent of wet loam, the parched earth's pungent odour of satiation only made Isobel's emptiness more acute.

Emma, too, was troubled. When Philip had initially been just *her* friend, it had all been perfect; but when he had become Mama's friend too it had all become somehow – frightening, as if Mama and Philip had stopped being friends with anyone else and were solely concerned with being friends with each other. It was then that Emma began to feel left out. And it was then, when she saw them together, that she wanted sometimes to scream and scream. But nobody else had seemed to notice, and so she had stayed silent. Only at night sometimes had she screamed, when in her dreams she saw Philip and Mama walk further and further away from her, laughing together, leaving her alone in a place that got progressively blacker the smaller their figures grew. It puzzled Emma that she was alone in her fear: it made it more frightening because no one else was frightened.

The day Philip left, Emma had felt her spirits lift in a timorous, shuddering way, as if after a long fit of crying. Now Mama would become Mama again, like she had always been. She would be released from the spell that appeared to have been cast over her and come back from wherever it was that she had seemed to go. But Mama was not very well that day, the day after the Jubilee fête, and had retired to her room after lunch with a headache. Emma hadn't wanted to go to the beach with the others. Instead she had stayed at home with Aunt Jude and had been allowed to bring her dolls downstairs with their cradles. She had made them a house behind the sofa, put them to bed and watched over them all afternoon. All the while she had kept one ear open for Mama's tread on the stairs, for she wanted to be the first to welcome her back, to hug her and hear her exclaim, 'Oh, Emma!' with the pleasure of seeing someone one is fond of, after a long absence. Perhaps, thought Emma, gazing at her sleeping dolls, it will take a bit longer; perhaps it will be like having the measles and Mama will have to get well gradually, day by day.

When eventually Isobel did descend to the drawing room, expecting to find only her aunt, she was startled to see Emma jump up from behind the sofa. She stood in the doorway, one hand on the knob, and stared at Emma with such paralysing mournfulness that Emma recoiled. If before nothing of Mama had looked out of Mama's eyes, in the split second that they stared at each other Emma now saw too much. She saw all the misery of being earthbound, of being consigned to a place where one no longer wished to be. And then her mother had quickly veiled her expression, passing her hand across her forehead as though to secure a mask, and walked over to Aunt Jude.

'I must have slept all this time,' she said dreamily. 'Shall we ring for tea?'

From then on things were different. Emma watched her mother constantly, to make sure her presence did not slip away again. And every time she looked into her mother's face, there was Mama, looking back at her. But it was not reassuring.

The restlessness, the glittering frustration, or the wide-eyed hopelessness that frequently overcame her were more than Emma could bear to watch. Mama might be with them, but it was not because she wanted to be; she was helpless to go anywhere else, however much she seemed to long to. She would sit on the beach and fan herself with her hat, then suddenly leap up and stride to the water's edge to pace up and down the shore, ignoring her daughters bathing in the shallows, staring past them far out to sea, with all the anguish of a fisherwoman in her eyes. Or she would wander round the garden at Quay House pulling every so often at some flower-head as she passed. Sometimes she became aware of Emma's wistful gaze and would sit with her on the sofa and read her a story, but she could never reach the end. Emma would hear her voice falter, slow, and stop. Mama, leaning back in her cushions, would close the book and smile apologetically: 'It's too hot to read, darling.' And Emma, confused and deserted, gave up adding new solutions for Mama's recovery to her bedtime prayers. In blank despair she accepted her mother's excuses and prayed fervently that the sun would stop shining.

Letters were rare at Walberswick, a fact that became, in the first few weeks of July, an obsession with Isobel. There was, she knew, the possibility of having them delivered three times a day. But days passed without there being anything, and when there was it was usually for Aunt Jude, who kept up a lively correspondence with her friends, exchanging embroidery patterns and boasting to each other of their grandchildren. Hiding her desperation as best she could, and feeling also that she should keep the arrival of the particular letter for which she craved secret from as many people as possible, Isobel would contrive to be alone as each delivery time approached. She would hover silently in one room or another, with the door open, listening, her heart thudding with anticipation, her mind empty and helpless. Sometimes the waiting would become too much and, unable to contain herself, Isobel would wander out into the hall or along the upstairs passages, darting back into an empty room if an unexpected noise from the rest of the house disturbed her. Then the expected hour for the postman would pass and her agitation would subside into listless despair.

As time went on and still no word came from Philip, Isobel began to feel increasingly confused, to doubt all those intuitions of which she had once felt so sure. They had said nothing to each other, she and Philip, for there had seemed no need for words, no need to express intentions that had seemed at the time so obvious. Only now, since she had been abandoned so abruptly and without any explanation, did doubt creep in. She could not believe Philip would not write to her, and yet she knew it was quite improper that he should. In this state of oscillation she craved even the smallest note from him to set her mind at rest. Perhaps, she would say to herself, it would be better if we never saw each other again, for nothing can come of it.

Then there were moods in which she would completely ignore the possible arrival of the post, spending the whole of the afternoon on the beach with her children, filled with a desire to hurt and ignore Philip, even in thought, to repay him for her own bewilderment. She would sit solidly and fiercely on the beach until, in the late afternoon, the image of a long white envelope with a French stamp in one corner lying on the hall table would so fill her mind that she could bear it no longer. She would insist on an immediate departure, striding across the beach followed by protesting children and a flustered maid festooned with hastily gathered rugs. The nearer she got to Quay House, the more certain Isobel felt that there would be a letter. The fact that she could picture it so clearly, lying on its silver tray on the sideboard in the hall, could even see the rectangular shadow that it cast over the polished oak, *must* mean that it existed, that it lay there, waiting for her. She would fling open the front door – and everything would crumble in the silence and emptiness of the hall. The only shadow that fell upon the polished oak was the circular rim of the small silver tray over whose empty surface the sunbeams danced heartlessly.

A letter came, as such things do, when Isobel no longer expected it. And, in the manner of so many important affairs, its delivery was given such special care that it got, not quite mislaid, but overlooked. To begin with, the postman arrived an hour early, as they had just begun lunch, and for some reason the maid who received the letter, instead of delivering it immediately, took it into the kitchen with the conceit in her head of serving it up as pudding: the importance of letters to their mistress was open gossip behind the green baize door, and the servants watched the post as avidly as she. But as the maid entered the kitchen to announce her prize, the scullery maid knocked over a pan of boiling potatoes with such loud screams that everyone in the room ran to her aid and the letter was dropped hastily among the pickle jars on the kitchen dresser, where it was forgotten in the chaos. In fact, it was the scullery maid herself who discovered the letter as she was tidying up after lunch. A kitchen conference was called, with much suppressed giggling, and it was decided that it might be politic to pretend the letter had come in the afternoon post, and to deliver it with tea.

The tea tray was generally set down in front of Aunt Jude, who enjoyed fussing over cups and saucers. They all saw the long envelope nestling between the teapot and the hot-water jug.

'Oh!' said Sophie and Maria together, and looked excitedly at each other, the subject of letters being one they discussed frequently in private, longing for the time of self-importance when letters should be addressed to themselves.

'Ah,' said Aunt Jude, picking up the envelope and reading the inscription.

'Another missive?' inquired Isobel, assuming it was for her aunt.

'A long-awaited missive,' replied her aunt, and held out the letter with an affectionate smile.

Isobel felt suddenly very hot. Her cheeks were flushed and her head buzzing, so that she could hardly hear her aunt's words. The envelope seemed to move unbelievably slowly towards her outstretched hand.

'Patience rewarded, my dear,' beamed her aunt. 'He must be extremely busy . . . '

Isobel grasped the stiff paper – the relief of having it at last in her hands.

'Well,' she laughed, 'you know how it is with these – ' Then she stopped. She held the envelope as still as she could between her shaking fingers and with a great effort of will subdued the rage that made her want to rip envelope and letter in two. The

126

moment passed and left her paralysed with disappointment. She stared down at the paper in her hands, at the English stamp and the neat, familiar writing.

'Mama!' Sophie could contain herself no longer. 'Mama, let me open it!'

'Mama!' Maria jumped up from her chair, 'let *me*!'

But Sophie snatched up the envelope, and with the letter out of her hands Isobel was able to flex her immobile fingers into some gesture of assent, the diversion provided by Sophie and Maria allowing the moment of tears to come and go with nothing more disastrous than a temporary glistening of the eyes. By the time Maria had danced off to the safety of the far corner of the room with the letter, unfolded it, and commenced to read it out loud, Isobel had achieved, if not composure, then a quiet, sad sliding of all aspiration, all longing and all hope down some dark chasm that opened up inside her and then silently closed upon her treasures.

Papa was announcing his intention of joining them at the weekend.

Chapter Twelve

Isobel lay back in the chair, her hands resting on the arms, her head tilted slightly to one side as though she were watching for something through the gap in the curtains. The chair had been placed beside the bedroom windows, from which there was a superb view of the common stretching up to meet the heath in the direction of the railway line. One had to be eagle-eyed to catch a glimpse of the tiny branch-line train as it chugged over the moors between Southwold and Halesworth, although at certain times of the day one could hear the whistle as it approached Walberswick Halt, and see the trail of smoke move across the heath. But Isobel had ordered the curtains to be drawn against the afternoon sun. Her bedroom hovered in a kind of twilight, except where rebellious bars of sunlight pushed in at the edges of the curtains to streak across the polished floor or lie against the walls, fingers of white light seeming to search out the occupant of the room. One even reached the edge of her pillow – but they could not find her. For she was not, in a sense, anywhere where she could be found.

Over the past week she had discovered the existence of a private world. A world into which she might sink at will. A world of warm silence, marked only by her own whispered words, words crowding and hissing together that she heard herself speak before she fell back, for long periods, into floating silence. At first she could reach her world only when she was alone, but as the days progressed she found herself sliding into it even when in the company of others. Only a certain far-away look on her face betrayed her absence, or an inability to answer questions whose words she heard but whose sense was meaningless to her. The impinging of the everyday world on her before she was ready to return to it irritated Isobel. She found its insistent demands for her presence tiresome. The rituals about which the people around her charted each day appeared, from Isobel's new vantage point, unbearably banal. The peaks of industry and excitement provided by meals and visits, dressing and duties, all levelled out into a desert of unending dreariness prickled with cactuses and littered with stones. Through this she saw her aunt and daughters and maids scurry and flap, like chickens without heads, quite unaware of where they really were or what was happening to them. She thought of the questions, the endless petty decisions, the small conferences they held one with another all day long over this or that. 'There are no decisions,' she whispered to herself, staring out of the gap in the curtains to where an inch of common shimmered in the late afternoon sun, crossed by a white track. 'There are no decisions to be taken any more.'

It was some time later that a door banging in the hall below roused her. Footsteps clattered on the stairs, neared her door and then receded. From one of the bedrooms, occasional high-pitched shrieks and cascades of giggles rippled away into the silence. After a while the stairs began to creak again, slowly and rhythmically. The footsteps approached her door, followed by light, tapping sounds like small patent-leather shoes on wooden boards. It was Aunt Jude and Emma. Isobel closed her eyes and feigned sleep, but their deliberation was momentary and unspoken. She heard them turn away without knocking and their footsteps vanished into Aunt Jude's room. Isobel slowly opened her eyes: Emma, deprived of her mother's jewel-box, would be allowed to play with Aunt Jude's, who would tell her stories about all the little cousins she never saw.

This, thought Isobel, is how the blind pattern their days, and she knew, from the stirrings of the house, that very soon she would be dragged back into the world of the sighted. She stretched in her chair and moved her hands, flexing her fingers, looking about her for something that might catch her attention and pull her slowly into action. The whole house, she knew, was simmering with excitement over the arrival that evening of her husband. Sophie and Maria were preening themselves in their best dresses, Emma and Aunt Jude were choosing layer upon layer of beads, the house shimmered with polish and glowed with roses, and she . . . she . . .

'Oh God,' she sobbed, and covered her face with her hands.

Light steps bounced from stair to stair, paused for a second on the landing as though to beat time and danced up the remaining flight to stop outside Isobel's door.

'Good evening, ma'am. Nancy curtsied in the doorway. 'You didn't ring, but I thought perhaps you'd forgotten the time.' She bustled across the room, and the room seemed to shrink back from her into its dusty corners. ''Tis neither night nor day in here, ma'am! Shall I light the candles?' She smiled across at Isobel, and it looked in the gloom as though she peered.

Embarrassed, Isobel bent her head. 'Yes, yes,' she said, and wondered what words she could add to appear more responsive to her maid's good humour. She could think of nothing; instead she got, a little unsteadily, to her feet, and once standing thought how futile a gesture it was: Nancy would only want her to sit down again. Nancy turned from lighting the candles with flames dancing in her eyes and flushed cheeks. She went over to the wardrobe, coming back with a length of pale blue silk and lace over one arm. She laid it over the back of the chair, and going round behind Isobel began to unhook her dress with such speed and dexterity that Isobel, still in a state of inertia, was taken completely by surprise.

'They're all so excited ma'am,' she began. 'Little Miss Maria and Miss Sophie . . . '

Isobel, warmed by the familiarity of the dressing ritual, watched in a frame of the candle-lit mirror how her dress uncurled from her shoulder like the shell of a chrysalis, exposing the pale skin beneath. But when she was seated again in her chair, wrapped in her blue peignoir, the moment came that she had been dreading, when Nancy's chatter ceased and she stood before the wide-flung doors of the wardrobe as though before Aladdin's cave, her hands folded demurely against her apron, her eyes shining with anticipation. Nancy expected it to be a happy occasion, this family reunion. They had prepared for it all week below stairs, and the culmination of it, in her eyes, was to be her dressing of the mistress.

'She'll be prettier than a picture!' she had boasted to Dolly as they laid the dining table together late that afternoon. She had stood back and surveyed the half-set table.

'I can just see her — sitting there in the candlelight, pale and serene . . . '

'Peaky, I'd call it,' Dolly had countered, laying out the glasses. 'She's sickening for something.'

'She's missing him.'

130

'Yes!' Dolly's look was arch, but Nancy ignored it.

'What's she going to wear?'

'She hasn't said.' Nancy picked up a handful of fish-knives. 'If I had my way, I'd have her in the pink.'

'Well, ma'am?' asked Nancy breathlessly, turning from the wardrobe. Isobel smiled wanly and waved a hand listlessly in the air. If only, she thought desperately, if only she could make herself care. But she couldn't.

'You choose,' she said, and let her hand drop.

'Well, ma'am' – Nancy seemed quite undismayed – 'if it was me . . .'

She dived into the wardrobe and emerged with the pink dress over her arms. Isobel stared at it in silence. Nancy shook out the train, and the tiny silk rosebuds rustled and swayed against each other.

'I don't know,' began Isobel, 'I don't know . . . what else is there?'

The pile of dresses on the bed grew and Nancy's good humour dissolved to the point of tears. There were more dresses in that wardrobe than Nancy and her sisters possessed between them. There was more money lying in coloured heaps on the end of the bed than her father had earned in his whole life. And all this stupid, spoilt woman had to do was choose one of them to wear. Her arm ached from holding out evening dresses for Isobel's inspection and her patience was worn thin by the fluttering silence with which each new suggestion was received. Nancy threw the last dress on the bed and then, alarmed by her own outburst of temper in the presence of her mistress, quickly picked it up again and began to twist the lace collar between her fingers.

'I wish,' came a harsh whisper from the chair, 'that they were all black!'

For a moment both women stared at each other in alarm.

'I mean,' continued Isobel, quickly, 'so that one wouldn't have to make a choice at all.'

'There don't have to be no choice, *really*, ma'am. They all look pretty,' said Nancy, trying to make amends.

Isobel smiled weakly. 'Bring me the pink.'

One could not stay in an enchanted world for ever, where dresses and jewels were irrelevant. Not if one drew one's substance from the other world, the real world. She must not stay so long in her private world again, she thought, as Nancy slipped the dress over her head. She must be careful, she mused, staring at her reflection in the mirror as Nancy coiled her hair in shining loops. She ran one finger over the moonstones that Nancy fastened round her neck: they were like soft oysters caught in a lace of silver seaweed. She must be this cold, this opaque; she could slip off now and then and let the waters close over her head, but she must not be seen. She had been careless over the past week in her relief at finding an escape from the bleakness. She must not be so again.

Thus Mr Heatherington returned to the bosom of his family and took up the role of master of the house. With a mixture of fear and excitement the maids smoothed their aprons, twisted their curls and said what a good thing it was to have a man round the house again.

'Master said to tell you it was quite delicious,' announced Dolly to the kitchen at large as she brought the fish-plates back from the dining room later that evening. 'And even Madam smiled! As for Miss Maria and Miss Sophie,' she continued, taking up the gigot of lamb from Mrs Freestone, 'they're fair got up tonight. Little pearl necklaces and little pearl bracelets, you'd think they were dining with their beaus!'

'You keep your thoughts to yourself, Dolly Brown,' snapped Cook, 'and don't drop that dish!'

Having inspected the house, inspected the cooking, inspected his wife, his children and his aunt by marriage, Reginald Heatherington sank contentedly into one of the armchairs by the fireplace in the drawing room. He rested his elbows on the arms of the chair, placed the tips of his fingers together with slow exactitude and, leaning his chin against them, surveyed the room before him. The lamps had been lit and the curtains drawn while they were at dinner; in the soft light the velvets and the Turkey carpets glowed gently and the features of the women who sat, one might say, at his feet were moulded with shadow and warmth. They were sufficiently far away from him, Isobel on the other side of the fireplace and her aunt next to her in the corner of an adjacent sofa, for a detached observation to be possible. They were engaged in some conversation about

Isobel's nieces, a discussion in which Reginald had no interest. He found instead that his mind had slipped involuntarily into its habit of 'totting up'. Gazing about the room, he placed thousand upon thousand with the dexterity with which one might build card houses.

They had taste, the owners, whoever they were. He had taste, too; he prided himself on his good taste. His house in London could stand comparison with many. But these people had something else, a something more enviable than good taste, something that showed in the family portraits and the perfectly faded carpets from Asia and China that lay across the polished floor. It was a very superior sort of summer-house. Pity no one in London could see it. Perhaps he'd have some of them down one weekend. There must be duck shooting along the marshes and soon there would be partridge. His eyes rested now on Aunt Jude and Isobel, and behind his fingertips his lips drew back over very white teeth in a curling smile. What was it they said about a good woman – a pearl that has no price? Course they had a price, they all had a price. He'd done well with these two, got them at a knock-down price, you might say. The aunt, for all her great bulk and her flashing beads, was like the owners of this house, whoever they were – she had not only refinement, she reeked of Family. She had Ancestry, nephews and great-nieces sprawled about the country. He liked that. He more than liked it, he craved it. He craved it now. It was part of his desire for Isobel; perhaps it was all his desire for Isobel, the thought of mingling his blood with hers. Beautiful, biddable Isobel. He could remember the night he had met her. He was just being introduced on the fringes of Society at that time as a young man who might go far in the City. He was spending far too much on clothes and a good address to impress the servants and the mothers in the various houses to which he was beginning to be invited. He had been introduced to Isobel's mother first, had stood being grilled by her for quite some time in a subtle but definite way, when this young girl had come up and stood demurely in front of them in her long white dress and her little pearl necklace. And Reginald had decided at that moment to acquire her. He could remember, with amusement, how her mother, in a somewhat irritated way, had tried to push her back into the fray and then, recollecting the young man at her side, had instead, introduced them. Behind the tips of his manicured fingers Reginald smiled again, and as if she sensed that the smile was directed at her, Isobel looked up at him. 'Aunt Jude is telling me such a funny story,' she said, as though apologising to him, and turned away again. Behind his fingertips Reginald's smile died slowly. Something in her face, something in her voice, something in the way she had raised her index finger to say she would give him all her attention in another quarter of a minute – something indefinable made him, momentarily, feel like a stranger.

He rose early the next morning. He rose and dressed and rang for shaving water; and while he stood and waited he flung open one of the bedroom curtains, throwing blinding sunshine on to Isobel's pillow. He stared moodily out at the view of garden and heath, vivid under the unrelenting sun. Isobel, caught in the glare of light, writhed and burrowed deeper into the sheets, feeling she was being torn out of sleep far too early. She heard the maid return with the water. She heard Reginald ask her if the children were awake. She heard the razor rasp across his chin and chink against the side of the shaving mug, the sounds of drawers softly opening and closing, the discreet clatter of bottles and brushes on the dressing table. Without speaking to her, her husband left the room. A little later she heard the children troop downstairs, and then sleep overcame her once more.

When later she woke, she lay and searched desperately in her mind for ways of escape. There could not be a repetition of the night before: his hands sliding over her, grasping her, pulling at her nightdress, and then the tears in the darkness. She thought of having the bed made up in one of the spare rooms, but there was no believable pretext either for sleeping in it herself, or banishing her husband to it. Nothing that would help her next weekend, or the weekend after, or the rest of the year, or all the years to come. She passed a hand across her face as though to banish the spectre of such a life sentence. She must do nothing to arouse his suspicions. Nothing. She must not cry again; she could not think why she had done so. It was her wifely duty to submit. It was . . . it was . . . *nothing*. She pulled at the lace edging of her pillow. She must have been affected by the wine at dinner. Or the heat. This eternal heat.

She could not remember so many hot days one after the other.

'It was nothing,' she whispered to herself, and smoothed out the sheet across her lap, as though trying to smooth out the furrows of her life. And then, swamped by a wave of panic, she flung back the bedclothes, reached for her wrap, and tugged violently at the bell-rope to ring for her maid. Standing by the bedhead she listened for Nancy's footsteps, but heard only the utter silence of the house. It was like a huge hollowness in which her room hung suspended, herself the only inhabitant. They were all gone. Her husband, her children, even Aunt Jude. She ran her hands over her arms as though seized by sudden cold, and in her mind's eye saw them, out there, on the sand. Walking, talking. Questions and answers. What else would they talk about but her. She saw the sly knowingness of Maria and the confused pain in Emma's eyes that she had deliberately ignored. She should have got up when they did, breakfasted with them, gone out with them; instead she had allowed herself to drift back to sleep, pushing away from the physical presence of her husband in the bedroom, back to the safety of unconsciousness. She shook her head, amazed at her own stupidity. He must know by now how far she had deviated from the brisk routine of their London household, how deeply she had plunged into irresponsibility. He despised indolence. Guiltily, she pulled her wrap tighter over her nightdress.

There came a soft knock at the door and she turned suddenly in her prowling round the bedroom carpet. Nancy entered, manoeuvring a breakfast tray through the doorway, balancing on one leg to close the door behind her.

'Why, ma'am!' Her smile faded as she caught sight of her mistress, not drowsily propped up against the pillows as usual, but standing at the foot of the bed clutching her robe, her face pale, her eyes glittering with alarm. 'I . . . I brought you your breakfast, ma'am,' holding out the tray like a tidbit to some wild animal.

'No, no!' Isobel's fright dissolved into anger. 'Not here!' She flapped her arms frantically at the tray. 'Bring me my clothes!'

Without a word Nancy set down the tray on the dressing table, went over to the wardrobe, opened the doors and stood respectfully to one side. Isobel turned on her heel. 'Anything,' she snapped.

She was dressed in the hard, spiked silence of unexpressed rage, both she and her maid so practised in the ritual that in spite of her temper the muslin floated fresh and summery around her and the curls at her neck hung in a collusion of softness. During it all, Isobel framed question after question in her mind about the absence of her husband and children, but as none of them seemed sufficiently nonchalant, her pride refused to allow her to utter any of them. In the silence her anxiety increased until she could sit still no longer, and snatching up her hat she swept out of the room. Nancy scurried after her with the tray.

At the foot of the stairs, Isobel sailed on towards the dining room. At the door she turned and saw Nancy heading in the direction of the kitchen.

'In here!'

'But the coffee needs warming, ma'am.'

Isobel shook her head. 'Not now.'

Inside the dining room Isobel hovered by the table watching Nancy set the tray down and begin to lay a place for her mistress.

'No, no,' muttered Isobel, almost to herself. Nancy stopped what she was doing. Isobel wandered uncertainly across the room, gazing around her. She caught sight of the table and chairs out on the terrace and opened the garden door. 'Quickly – out here!'

It was where Aunt Jude liked to spend her mornings with Mr Smytheson, but this morning it was deserted. Isobel sat in one of the chairs, but the sun squinted too much into her eyes and she felt she did not face the door to the dining room at quite the best angle. She jumped up and sat in another chair, brushing the palms of her hands across the table-top in front of her as though clearing away imaginary debris. Nancy laid down the tray without unloading it. Her mistress stared at it in silence, smoothing out her skirts, and then said in a low voice, 'Pour me some coffee and then take the pot away.'

Nancy stepped back with the half-empty coffee pot in her hand. Isobel fingered the tiny pearl necklace round her throat and nervously straightened the muslin ruffles of her collar. 'And take one of the rolls away.'

Nancy approached the table again and stared bewildered at the small bread roll. There was no spare plate on which to carry it away, no instrument with which to pick it up. She could think of nothing to do and so, agitatedly, she moved the coffee pot from her right to her left hand.

'I can't, ma'am.'

'Remove it!' hissed Isobel. She wanted all evidence of breakfast, all sight of this silly, hesitating girl, to be gone. She wanted to be left alone to compose herself; she wanted to be alone when they returned. Nancy grabbed the roll, tried to curtsey, overbalanced, spilled coffee down her apron as she did so, and fled to the kitchen.

Isobel heard them first in the hall. There was a burst of sound which faded and then, as she quickly slid her buttery plate out of sight under the saucer of her coffee cup, renewed itself with the opening of the dining-room door. Emma, Sophie and Maria trooped across the room and out on to the terrace, followed by their father. They settled around Isobel like a flight of pigeons, balancing on the backs and arms of chairs, cooing and fluttering at her.

'You've been away hours,' cried Isobel gaily. 'I thought you'd never come. I've even had my morning coffee. Reggie – ' she tilted her face up to her husband, who lounged against the open French window watching them, 'won't you ring for Nancy to bring you a cup?'

'Just made it, has she?'

'Well,' Isobel pouted, and lifted one of her hands to indicate the passing of an unspecified length of time.

Emma, leaning over the back of one of the chairs, wondered, because everyone seemed to be smiling at everyone else, whether it would be a good moment to ask if she might have just half a small spoonful of jam. But as she opened her mouth to speak, it occurred to her that if it were morning coffee, then why was there a tiny silver dish of jam on the tray. She looked across at Mama, who was turning from person to person as they spoke in the most animated way. Emma saw the pearls round her neck glint in the sunshine and noticed that she smelt of more scent than usual. She wondered why her mother was so dressed up today; perhaps they were going to have a special lunch, like the special dinner they had had last night. She mused on this compensatory possibility for a while and then turned her attention to her sister. Sophie was describing their return across the marshes, over the high bridge and up into the village.

'Capital marshes,' interjected Papa, and his teeth glinted white under his moustache as he grinned. 'Good bit of duck shooting, I shouldn't wonder. Could be fun, eh?'

'There aren't any ducks,' Emma said, in a small, cold voice.

'No ducks? Rubbish!' He opened the palm of one hand: 'Marsh.' He opened the other palm: 'Ducks.' He clapped them together: 'Stands to reason.' And he rubbed his hands, seeing his stature in the city enhanced by feathers.

'Mr Steer said so,' the little voice continued.

'Gamekeeper is he?'

'Mr Steer doesn't shoot things, he paints them,' Emma retorted.

'Knows all about birds, then!' Reginald was pleased to see Sophie and Maria's smirks had dissolved into giggles, but Isobel looked dashed odd and little Emma seemed near to tears.

Lunch was not the special affair that Emma had hoped for. The talk was desultory and centred mainly on Mr Smytheson, his house, the other houses in the village and their comparison with Quay House, although according to her father, none of them could possibly compare.

'We've got the best of the bargain,' he concluded, and leaned back in his chair proprietorially.

When lunch was over and coffee had been cleared away, when the afternoon stretched long, blue and hot before them, a bored silence fell on the little group. The Walk had already been taken. The copy of The Times, whose leaves Papa turned so rapidly, contained news that he had read and re-read. An afternoon of playing on the beach did not seem to be in order.

'We could take a drive!' suggested Maria.

'We could have tea in the wood again,' added Sophie, brightening.

'Oh, no,' replied Isobel quickly and then, recovering herself, added, 'we should have to order the chaise in advance.'

'Let's do it tomorrow. Send Mr Budge to order it for tomorrow!' begged Sophie.

Reginald closed the paper, folding it smaller and smaller until it was no more than a baton of newsprint. He began to tap it lightly and rhythmically to the refrain of the dance tune that ran in his head, and stared out across the garden. He'd had enough of this country family life, he'd give anything to be back on a train to London. To smell the acrid smoke of Liverpool Street Station and see the blackened houses closing in. To feel himself back in that crowded milieu where the sharpest card always took the trick.

The following day, they stood in little groups on the gravel path before the church porch, chatting after morning service. It was very hot. The sunlight beat off the small white stones among the gravel and the cut flints set into the walls of the church looked glassy. People seemed to hover in the dancing heat, like gnats. Some of them were waiting to meet Reginald; others were content merely to watch him. They stood a little way off from their more exalted neighbours idling among the gravestones near the path, or clustered round the lych gate. They saw how Isobel hung on her husband's arm in a drooping curve and remarked how pale her face was beneath the dark brim of her hat. He, on the other hand, seemed quite animated. He talked, he smiled, the dark head inclining quickly towards each new person, his hand extending itself towards each new hand and appearing to withdraw sharply on the point of contact as though he disliked the touch of strangers. From their positions of anonymity, the villagers watched him with the apparent indifference and the keen penetration with which they might observe the habits of some small animal. They fitted him into the history they had already amassed for him, a history constructed, like most of their knowledge, on a mixture of hearsay and observation. They were impressed, but not deceived, by his air of wealth; they admired, but did not altogether envy him, his beautiful wife; and they wished their own children had the straight limbs, full bellies and bright eyes of his daughters. When, eventually, he called his family to him and led them away from the church on to the road, they stood casually aside for him to pass, as though turning on their own account to some important, private business. And as he walked at the head of his little brood, so in ones and twos they followed him, moving off silently behind him, still with the same air of blank indifference. They passed Mr Smytheson's house, they passed the almshouses where old men stood among cabbages and hollyhocks and watched them go by. They passed the windmill among the pine trees and came up to the village green. Gradually, in ones and twos, the villagers dropped out of the procession. One might have said that they did so for the most natural of reasons: because they had reached home, or encountered a neighbour. Or perhaps they left, each of them, at the precise moment that they had the measure of their quarry. They had taken his scent and marked his pace; for the present they need track him no further.

By the time they reached the brow of the slight hill that led down to the quay, the Heatheringtons were, at last, alone. They had been quite silent as they walked through the village; it was only now, as they descended the slope, that they spoke. A small puff of wind blew up from the estuary, catching at Isobel's hat.

'Oh!' she exclaimed, and lifted her hand from her husband's arm to catch hold of the brim. He watched her, staring into her face.

'You're very pale.'

She tried to smile lightly, to turn away his probing eyes, but he did not smile back at her.

'I'm concerned. Your aunt says you find this heat a great trial.'

'Everyone finds this heat a great trial,' she replied, quickening her pace. 'Don't you, in London?'

They were at the garden gate now. She put out her hand to open it and escape from him into the house, but his own hand moved faster, and he held the gate closed against her.

'No,' he said quietly, 'I don't.'

Then the others were all around them and he was forced to let her go.

Inside the house, Isobel went quickly upstairs to take off her hat. But Reginald followed her to her room, entering so quietly as she sat at the mirror staring at her reflection, her hat in her hands, that she realised someone else was there only when she heard the soft click of the door. He sat on the bed behind her, staring solemnly at his wife's reflection in the mirror.

'Are you sure you want to stay here right till the end of the summer?' he asked.

The face in the glass nodded at him. 'Oh, yes,' it smiled. 'The children would never forgive me . . . '

'I wasn't thinking about the children.'

The eyes in the mirror widened. He thought they almost laughed at him. 'I love it too!'

'Those people we met after church,' continued Reginald, as though approaching the problem from another angle, 'are they your only society?'

'Not quite,' said Isobel defensively.

There was a pause, and then a hand appeared in the mirror, its fingers spread out. 'There's the doctor and his wife, who live in Dunwich' – two fingers curled into the palm of the hand – 'and the Colonel and *his* wife' – two more fingers curled away, leaving only the thumb standing. In the silence the thumb waggled about rather awkwardly. 'Oh! And of course, Aunt Jude; it's wonderful to have her to myself for a whole summer.' Isobel prattled on for fear of what her husband might say should she allow a silence.

Below them in the hall the gong boomed for lunch. Out of habit Reginald stood up. She could no longer see his eyes in the mirror, but she knew he watched her still.

'Invite them over next time I'm down.'

It was more a command than a suggestion, but it seemed to indicate that the conversation was ended. And then, as an afterthought, like some name missed off a guest list, Reginald added, 'What about the painter?'

The mirror was obscured by a wide expanse of blue silk as Isobel rose suddenly to her feet.

'He's gone. He apparently comes down every summer to paint for a few weeks – and then goes.' She walked towards the door and looked back over her shoulder at him; the movement twisted her neck a little, and her mouth. It was difficult to be sure that she was smiling. 'Shall we go to lunch?' she said softly, and then quickly turned away from him again and left the room.

Chapter Thirteen

Isobel sat in the garden on a wicker chaise-longue, her whole body flung out and loose along its length, her eyes half-closed. Beside her on the terrace sprawled Emma, cutting out paper dolls in silent concentration, her scissors the only sound in the still garden, a small, determined rasping as the paper curled and fell away before them. Sophie and Maria were on the beach, her aunt was out visiting and her husband had left for London the evening before. The household was settling back into its accustomed pattern of life after the excitement of the weekend and Isobel lay in the garden as though recovering from an intense and arduous ordeal. She felt as if she had narrowly escaped some awful danger and had reached safe ground again, as if she had been running and running and had flung herself down here panting and had only just got her breath back. But with the sense of relief came a cold, creeping certainty that the respite was limited. However well she had played her part over the weekend, it had not been enough. She had felt her husband watching her constantly, sensing that she had changed and not being able to pinpoint how or why. He would return, the scrutiny would begin again, and on the slightest pretext he would order her back to London.

At most, she mused, she had another month of independence. A month in which to be alone, or, rather, not alone – one was never quite that – but with people who let one be oneself. She had never, she realised, really been allowed to be herself; there had always been people who dominated her with their own rules and expectations. She had not even been aware that she was being dominated, or that she had a self to explore, a self that might want different things. Now she had discovered it, but the discovery seemed to have come too late. She felt like a dying man discovering the secret of life too late to put it into action, who half-lifts himself from his pillows and calls out to death, 'Wait! Wait! I know how to do it now!'

A month, perhaps not even a month. It was like giving a

condemned prisoner a month of freedom and sending him home to make his farewells. What would he do? Would he call in all his friends and relations and declare 'open house' for the last four weeks of his life? Or would he sit in some corner alone, feeling the sun warm against his skin, staring at a blade of grass with an unassuageable ache of bitterness and deprivation, swamped by his sense of loss, envying the blade of grass the fact that its life would be a day longer than his. If he had any sense, thought Isobel, the prisoner would try to escape. She would have done that, if only . . .

She stared out across the garden, but instead of bitterness she suddenly felt only how precious these last weeks were. It occurred to her that she had never really looked at the garden properly before: it was not just a static backdrop, it had an intense life of its own. The more she gazed, the more a feeling of weightlessness overcame her; she heard the hum of bees approach and recede like waves, and the finches fighting in the pear trees with a commotion of clicking leaves and shrill cries. The last of the summer flowers, standing in drifts of fallen petals, their perfume desiccated into a premature musk of decay, appeared suddenly exquisitely beautiful. Colour and sound seemed to ripple across the space towards her. All she had to do was to sit very still and it would come to her, like a long-awaited answer to some puzzling question. It was so simple she felt like laughing out loud. Perhaps, she thought, the answer is not to hide away from life, but to hide in life. Out here, in this enchanted garden, where all is noise and colour and warmth. But what would she do when winter came? Where would she hide when the grass was shorn with frost and the trees dark and awkward in their nakedness? The enchantment would not last. Everything died. She would have died too, she thought impassively, by then. When autumn came, she would be taken away from here to live on like a dead person. She would never be allowed to go away like this again; not until years had passed and life had become meaningless and aimless; not until all desires and expectations had withered away. Only when she no longer craved freedom would she be given it. All she would have to sustain her would be memories fixed to this place, like ghosts.

If it were true that ghosts returned to inhabit the scenes of great emotional events in their lives, then perhaps this terrace where she sat was, in fact, bustling with shapes treading out their past again, flagstone by flagstone, unaware of all the others doing the same thing, moving through each other and past each other without the slightest displacement of matter. 'Perhaps this garden is full of people I don't see,' said Isobel to herself. But in her mind she saw only Philip. 'Perhaps this terrace is crowded with people who nod and smile and drink tea and talk of the weather and sip wine. Perhaps somewhere among them is a young couple who think themselves entirely alone among this whispering throng.' She closed her eyes the better to see, and all the bitter-sweet anguish of being with Philip again, even in the remotest way, rose up to cloud her vision.

'And the living,' thought Isobel, 'are their hearts never drawn by the memory of periods of great emotion to relive such moments of intensity? When we walk round all day thinking of someone who is not there; when, in our imaginations, we conjure up memories of exactly how they looked and talked, of the places in which we saw them, even of the way we ourselves felt and what we did and said in reply, is not some ghostly fragment of ourselves flying off to relive its happiness? Might not Philip think of this place? Might he not return in spirit to everywhere that we have been together?' Fleetingly, she saw again the waiting figure among the sand-dunes, watching for her from the marshes, hovering round the pier, racing down the road to the quay clutching his hat in one hand and his painting gear in the other. The first shy emotions of their meetings; the drives, the teas, the fête at Dunwich. And now the emptiness. But perhaps in essence he was here still. Fragments of him, like torn threads from a coat caught on a gorse bush, in every place that he had ever been. Even the places he had painted – maybe more there than anywhere else, for two passions would be running side by side to press his imprint further against the backdrop of that place.

'He *is* here,' whispered Isobel breathlessly, caught up in the logic she had spun for herself. 'I can be with him still, until the end of summer!' A great surge of energy flooded her and an impatience at lost opportunities, as though Philip had been waiting for her out on the heath all these weeks and she had not known that he was there. She sat up quickly and a blackbird which had been hopping close to her chair stared up at her out of its round, black eye, startled, and flew off screaming across the lawn. Isobel looked down at her daughter, snipping imperturbably round the head of a doll.

'Come on,' said Isobel, 'let's go and walk across the marsh and surprise Sophie and Maria from the sand-dunes.'

'I thought we weren't going down to the beach till tea.'

'Are you too busy cutting out?'

Emma squinted up at her mother. 'It's too hot to go for a walk.'

Isobel laughed, bending down to stroke back the ends of hair that had fallen over Emma's face. 'Come on!'

So it was almost every day from then on. Just as the heat was finally beginning to wear away those around her, Isobel seemed to take on new energy. She wanted, constantly, to go for walks. She sent one of her maids every other day to engage the chaise for a drive. She would take anyone with her on these excursions who would come, as though companions were an unimportant formality. For she was going, in reality, alone. The jaunts took on a serious intensity, as if they had great purpose, although Isobel never quite seemed to know where she was going until she got there. She would parry requests from her companions to go to a particular place with deliberate vagueness, just to entice them to accompany her. Once their journey had begun she would take over, scenting her way like a bloodhound each time their path forked, choosing this one rather than that on pure instinct, her eyes dancing and her face alight with pleasure. Reaching some spot significant only to herself, she would spread her arms with a contented smile, brushing her fingers over bleached grasses and desiccated gorse bushes, or sink to the ground and sit for a long time staring out in front of her in abstracted silence, until the fidgeting of her bored companions roused her.

July faded into August, but Isobel's passion for excursions did not abate. Aunt Jude soon learned to excuse herself from these jaunts, but Sophie, Maria and Emma were captive.

They would clamber into the chaise silently and shuffle on the cushions. Their silence was part lethargy, part familiarity: there was nothing to discuss. They sat always in the same

145

places. Only once, long after the little girls had discovered the pointlessness of requesting a particular destination, did Emma say, as the chaise lurched forward over the gravel driveway, 'Do let's go somewhere cool,' in a voice of such stoical suffering that her mother turned to her with surprise and concern.

'Why, my darling, by all means, let's go to Foxburrow Wood.'

Surprised by their unexpected success, the sisters smiled at each other, wriggled on their seats, patted at their hats and generally tried to infuse some anticipation of pleasure into the journey. They drove out of the village and on to the heath, bravely holding their heads up as the stifling air rolled over the dried heather and lifeless gorse, half-closing their eyes to it and firmly shutting their mouths against the dust raised by the pony's hooves. When finally they dropped down the hill into the plantation of young firs they felt almost excited, but then, as the woods rose up tall and dark, unaccountably their spirits plummeted. Clouds of gnats appeared and hovered over the pony's steaming flanks. His head dropped lower than ever and the driver, hunched over the reins in such a way that one could not tell whether he were asleep or awake, made no attempt to raise it.

As if by intuition, the pony stopped in front of the clearing where, long ago, they had had their picnic. Instead of coolness and greenness, heat seemed to radiate out of the pines, mixed with a strong scent of resin, as though the trees themselves were melting and running away across the floor of the forest. The predominant colour seemed to be brown, a light grey-brown, a brown that you could rub into dust between your fingers. There was dust in the shafts of sunlight trapped between the rows of trees, dust spinning slowly through air thickened with millions of other particles, past broken branches and peeling tree-trunks to land in stifling heaps beneath the trees. They stared in silence, none of them making the slightest move to climb down from the chaise, as though fearing that if they stepped on to this enchanted place they too might shrivel like the grass. Instead they sat, watching in their memories the ghosts of young girls as they danced along soft green rides between the trees, and of a man and a woman who sat for ever in a sunlit clearing close enough to touch each other.

Isobel gazed until she could bear it no longer and then ordered the driver to turn the pony's head for home. The presence of the place was too strong for all of them, and no one ever again suggested that they return.

From then on, Isobel confined their drives to the immediate area around the village, giving directions from her vantage point behind the driver's left shoulder, as though by sudden and divine inspiration.

'Give me a party as knows their own mind,' the driver would grumble to his wife after these outings, as he rubbed his sweating pony down. 'All this turn right and turn left, and "Let's see what's down this liddle lane, Mr Jonas." Give me a party as says, "Drive me to Southwold," and leaves the way to me. 'Tain't no point their paying me to drive and then tryin' to do it theirself!' But it was the thought of the payment that made him turn up at Quay House promptly every time Isobel sent for him.

Maria, Sophie and Emma also came to see these drives as something to be endured. They enjoyed at first the excuse to change their clothes and put on hats, to be paraded round the village and out into new countryside. But as the newness faded and they came to notice that only small children and dogs ran out to watch their passing, and that every journey led nowhere, they lost interest. Whichever direction they took they saw the same burnt grass and dusty grey hedgerows curled in on themselves. They drove past fields where trees seemed to sway in the heat holding up bare branches dried white almost to cracking point. In one meadow a tree stood gaunt and alone in the midst of an empty field. In another, a group of trees gathered ghost-like in a corner, looking as though one push would knock them over to splinter, hollow-trunked, against the hard ground. Always the drive ended with the sudden halting of the chaise, the dazed descent, the resigned drooping of the pony's head, the sullen disapproval of the driver's hunched back and the quick, excited footsteps of their mother as she followed them.

'Look,' she would say, 'at the view!' And they would politely squint from under the brims of their hats at the parched landscape before them, to where the line of the sea, shimmering and winking, made them screw up their eyes even further.

They would tentatively lick the dust from their lips and slide hot fingers under the elastic on their hats where it had made tight, red bands across their necks.

Then, finally, came the occasion when Isobel halted the chaise in a lane high up on the heath, where the trees gave way to a clear view of the marsh, and on, out to where the sea lay along the line of the horizon. Deep ditches had been dug along the roadside, the clay thrown up on the far bank too high for anyone to jump it. Sophie, Maria and Emma stood around uncertainly, scuffling at the dried earth with their shoes, insinuating insuperable difficulties in going a step further.

'Come on,' said Isobel, climbing down from the chaise.

'Where?' muttered Sophie.

'Over the ditch and up on to the bank,' called Isobel.

'How?'

Isobel looked around her for some means of crossing the ditch. Further down, a broad plank had been thrown across the gap; mud-coloured, it could hardly be seen at first glance.

'Over there.' She waved a gloved hand. 'You go first,' she added, and turned to speak to the driver.

Sophie strode off, furious that she had failed to confound her mother's plans, bored with the whole, hot afternoon, and approached the plank bridge, not with the temerity one might have expected, but with all the blindness of rage. Sulkily, Maria followed her. It was Maria's footsteps, shaking the plank when Sophie was only halfway over, that made her turn to glare at her sister, and then to scream, and Maria, looking down at precisely the same moment, screamed too. The sisters, unable to move on and too terrified to stay where they were, performed a strange, tottering dance in the centre of the plank, clutching each other and screeching hysterically. Their exit from the bridge was blocked by Emma, who stared open-mouthed into the ditch. An old man lay there, fully clothed, his eyes shut; his face under its matted beard was grey, flies crawled at the corners of his open mouth. Without the least sign of movement, a soft, bubbling giggle rose from the body, grew louder and then trickled into silence.

On Aunt Jude's insistence, the drives were thereafter discontinued.

*   *   *

The doctor leaned back in his chair. 'It is despair,' he said. 'It is a certain sort of blankness, a kind of giving up, an abandonment, almost, to oblivion. I have been watching it for some time.' He paused reflectively. 'And you, too.' Dr Morris turned towards Reginald Heatherington with the sharply focused gaze of the medical man who has pondered not only the case of his patient, but seen through the confusion and pain of life itself to make his diagnosis. 'You must have noticed it on your visits down here. It must have struck you quite forcibly.'

'Well!' It was half a word, half a short laugh. Reginald squirmed a little in his chair. 'I don't get down here very often – not nearly as often as I'd like.'

He began to twirl the stem of his wine glass in his fingers, comforted by the reassuring glitter of light on the cut surface and the dark velvet of the wine within. He picked it up and drank, with an exaggerated slowness. There were, his gestures insinuated, more important things occupying his mind.

The doctor gazed thoughtfully past Reginald out through the window to where early shadows crept across the gilded evening grass. 'It sometimes happens,' he said slowly, as though moulding his thought for the first time, 'that a person struggling for too long against outside forces that are inimicable, too strong for them, can have his personality quite altered. Either it collapses under the strain, succumbing in blank obedience, or, in a desperate attempt to protect itself, it turns itself inside out, exhibiting traits the reverse of its normal character. Behind these, the poor, confused creature hides, as though waiting for a storm to pass, waiting for the return of life as he knew it hitherto. Waiting for the return of the old moralities, familiar faces now absent, familiar rituals and expectations once again to become his.' The doctor's voice had sunk very low with these last words. Now it lifted as he drew back his hunched shoulders and smiled at the serious faces around him. 'Death, love and progress' – he lifted his glass – 'tip mankind from his equilibrium more surely than any other natural disaster you care to name.' He swung round to face Isobel. 'It was progress you saw, Madam, lying dead drunk in a ditch the other day.'

Reginald wondered whether he should protest on behalf of his womenfolk; he looked down the table and saw, to his surprise, that they were smiling at the doctor. The doctor's wife, however, was smiling at *him*, or rather not quite smiling, observing him out of calm eyes as though he were a microbe under her husband's microscope. He felt suddenly out of it.

'You don't hold with progress, doctor,' he drawled.

The doctor put down his glass. 'Progress in this village and my own – in the whole of this county – is tearing families apart, turning good men and women into despairing, starving vagabonds. We are an agricultural county, Mr Heatherington. When large estates are ruined, the estate-worker is turned off the land. England may be flooded with cheap food, but this same man and his family, dispersed to mills in the nearest town, or gang-labouring on a far-off estate, will never see a bite of it. It has not nourished him; it has caused his downfall.'

'I see you don't approve of free trade either!' Reginald drew himself in as though expecting an insult. He had made a fortune on the free market.

'I see the evidence of it,' said the doctor softly, and then shook his head a couple of times as if to rid himself of the vision. 'If I did not, it would be a theory of economics I might very well support.'

'Britain is the supreme trading nation.' Reginald had decided to go into the attack. 'There's not a country in the world with whom we don't trade; a free market is a healthy market.'

The ladies sat quietly while the men sparred around them: a delicate, foil-tipped fencing match, all the more polite because each man despised what the other stood for. The ladies were not expected to join in. They sat in calm attitudes of respectful silence, with masks of interest on their faces. Aunt Jude, her eyes shining as black as the jet beads festooning her dress, her head turning from speaker to speaker, listened to all the familiar arguments, and thought of how many tables these same chestnuts had been rolled across, backwards and forwards. She had spent her life, she mused, sitting at other people's tables, until she had learned to become the perfect guest.

Further down the table, opposite her husband and next to Isobel, Emily Morris listened to the debate, with her head lowered and a light, fond smile playing along her mouth. She ran her forefinger over the delicate silver moulding on the handle of her dessert fork, tracing out the pattern of vine leaves and hard little clusters of grapes, and thought how proud she was of her husband's compassion. He would never have made a fashionable town doctor. They had come to Dunwich soon after they first married as an interim practice and had never left. Her friends had thrown up their hands in horror at her entombment. She had packed away all the boxes of wedding presents, the silver and the fine linen, and had been happier than she had ever thought it possible to be. They entertained rarely, because there was no one to entertain – except each other. Sometimes, even now, she would have the fire lit in the morning room and the small oval table laid with her finest china, and they would dine together in splendour and content-ment while the servants shuffled begrudgingly the extra length of passage with plates and dishes. And always, almost always, before the meal could be completed, one of them would come with a message that so-and-so was ill. Then the make-believe would collapse and she would be left sitting there in an old-fashioned dress watching the firelight play on the tall, engraved glasses and make cavernous shadows in the folds of the damask napkin abandoned by her husband. She had dessert-knives and forks very like these, wrapped carefully away in a velvet-lined box in one of the oak chests in the second spare bedroom. Imagine Isobel Heatherington having the same thing.

Isobel, unaware of Emily Morris's scrutiny, leaned her chin on her hand. She had been gazing down the length of the dining table, a polite smile on her face, without really listening to what either man said. Now, surreptitiously, she withdrew her gaze, winding it in like a silken thread, until it lighted on the strands of philadelphus and the pink rosebuds that had been fixed around the column of the silver candlestick nearest to her. The light of the candles hardly showed, for it was only about seven o'clock, but the delicate cream and blush of the flowers was accentuated by the setting sun, with a light so low that it seemed to come from within, glowing out of the heart of each flower. She stared at them, transfixed by one in particular which leaned out on its spray towards her, its lower petals curled in a waxy, creamy whiteness of perfection. The more she stared into it, the more its perfection seemed to express something absolute, some tangible answer to the doubt and anxiety of the past few weeks. She bent forward, struggling to decipher its message: if only she could be so sure, so perfect. And then, with a sound no louder than a puff of air, one of the white petals detached itself and fell on to the polished surface of the table. Isobel drew sharply back, the corners of her mouth twisted with distaste. But the petal looked as perfect as if it were still attached to the flower; there was no trace of decay, no mark or tear. Above it the flower, incomplete and decaying, hung as beautiful as ever.

The curtains had not been drawn in the dining room, but the high wall protected the occupants from any curious gaze. As the sunset flared along the horizon, the house glowed a burnt orange-red against the pale sand-dunes; then, suddenly, the light was extinguished and the landscape retreated into greys and blues. Quickly, or so it seemed to the man who sat among the ruins of the stonebreaker's hut on the common, the shadows crept from tree to tree; they hung from the gables of the house and underlined each jutting brick, until the face of the house was drowned in shadow. Shadows filled up the hollows of the old quarry and lay along the hedgerows. The trees of the spinney that ran between the common and the village merged slowly into one another, linking dry branches to protect the sleeping hamlet. He saw lights appear in some of the upstairs rooms of the house, but still he sat. Dogs barked occasionally from the village; little whirring moths passed his head. The twilight world was held in a creaking kind of silence, a stifling darkness, which gave scant respite from the dull heat of the day. He had retired into his dream, but it was not quite as he had dreamed it. He should not have come. But he could not have stayed away.

He had tried to miss the train earlier that evening, delaying and prevaricating, pretending not to notice the time, feeling each minute beat out its course inside his head. Until finally he had rushed out of the house in a panic. All of London had seemed deliberately to slow its pace around him, holding him back. His hansom cab was reduced to walking pace as they entered the City. It was the hour when the offices and banks closed, and against the flood of cabs disgorging from every thoroughfare progress had been impossible. In desperation Philip had abandoned his cab and leapt out into the surging tide of black-hatted, black-coated humanity, and had almost been drowned by it.

He had reached the station just before the departure of his train and managed to hurl himself into one of the last carriages, where he lay slumped on the seat, hatless and ticketless. But the pounding in his heart did not subside for the whole journey. At times he would sit staring at the floor of the carriage, thinking what an utter fool he was making of himself in embarking on this journey, unable to bring himself even to look out of the window, so deeply did he feel he disgraced himself. At other times he would leap up in a frenzy, pacing the compartment, beside himself with inarticulate rage, once or twice scarcely managing to restrain himself from actually pulling the communication cord to stop the train.

His heart still pounded as he sat in the darkness on Walberswick Common, but the frenzy had subsided into a more practical anxiety: what on earth should he say to Isobel, what should he do, now that he was returned? He could not turn back. He was held fast even by the sight of her house, those wavering candle-lights set along the staircase, the single glow in one of the bedrooms above. He sat on in the darkness.

Some time later there was a burst of noise from the direction of the house as a door opened. Voices rose and died away, rippling out after each other. A moment later he heard horses' hooves and caught a glimpse of a swaying light along the road in front of Quay House. The sound faded to reappear a minute or so later, behind and parallel to where he sat, as the pony emerged from the village, passed the church and disappeared out on to the heath road. Philip sat on. He wondered who might have visited her, and watched the lights in the house as they were extinguished, one by one.

Flying out, as it were from the house itself, bats dived and shrieked across the common, scraps of darkness in the pale night air, playful as swallows round his head. From the copse floated a barn owl, scattering the bats, hunting low over the ground, as undisturbed by Philip's presence as if he did not exist, sailing on towards the heath where fieldmice hid under gorse bushes. He walked down towards Quay House and stood uncertainly beside the garden wall, his feet in a clump of dead nettles, one hand against the bricks. They were still warm to the touch, still reverberating with heat, rough and porous, a honeycomb of air and rose-coloured sand. 'A wall of spun sugar,' he mused, smiling to himself in the darkness, 'behind which lies the prize of fairy tales.'

He stepped back on to the common and walked quickly away across the grass towards the opening on to Quay Road. Not now. Tomorrow morning. He felt relieved to hear the solid security of the gravel rasp beneath his feet. Or tomorrow afternoon.

Chapter Fourteen

Philip could not bring himself to visit Isobel the next day. His landlady had invited him to join her for Sunday lunch in her parlour, and over the boiled mutton she gave him a detailed account of the morning service she had just attended. He waited eagerly for Isobel's name. But when it came it was coupled with her husband's, and his pride was instantly crushed.

'. . . so nice to see them all together again. Those pretty little girls, and her aunt here, too. Nice for them to have their Papa down for the weekend. More mutton, Mr Steer? No? They had the doctor and his wife from Dunwich over for dinner last night; I heard their trap go back through the village no more than twenty minutes before you came in. Mrs Freestone cooked them a baron of beef. They'll be having that cold for lunch today, I'll be bound. I do think a baron of beef's better cold than 'tis hot, don't you, Mr Steer? Little bit of relish and a nice pickled egg. Well, now!' She leaned perilously far back in her chair, groping for the bell-push to summon Agnes with their pudding. Philip thought unkindly of the wisdom of too much porter on a hot afternoon. 'And how long are we having you with us this time?' Mrs Pearce beamed at him, ladling gooseberry pie on to a white china plate. 'Them's me own!' she confided as Philip watched the berries tumble out of the pastry casing into a pool of syrup on his plate. He wanted to leave immediately.

'I'm not sure.' He took up his spoon and smiled hesitantly at his hostess. 'Is it inconvenient for you, about the room? Might there be other guests?'

'Lord love you, who'd want to come and stay down here in this desert!'

Philip took himself off after lunch with a sketchbook under his arm and a broad-brimmed hat on his head, striding fiercely across the iron ground, plunging down into the depths of the marshes, where only wild birds went because the land was usually so waterlogged. Here the mud had baked and cracked into sinister fissures, and everywhere hung the sulphurous smell of weed, long-submerged, drying in the heat. Philip did not return to 'The Anchor' until late that evening. The next morning he went off after breakfast, along the line of the sand-dunes, with sandwiches in his pocket and a stone bottle of cold beer slung over his shoulder. As on the day before, he found he could do no more than draw mechanically, page after page of reed-heads and flowers. From where he sat, in a hollow of the dune overlooking Town Marsh, he could survey the whole landscape of village, marsh and cornfields. He stared into it, taking pessimistic relish in its dusty, suffocated air of exhaustion. The lushness of late June and the bright colours were gone. Gone. Finished. He hissed the words with bitter pleasure through his clenched teeth.

After the departure of her husband Isobel felt, as always, a surge of energy and relief, the delight of being alone again in her private world. On Monday morning she accompanied her children to the beach. They went straight to the water's edge, and she went with them. The sea, oozing backwards and forwards over the sand, glinted maliciously in the hazed sunlight, offering only salt to the parched land. Soon the children were absorbed in their watery world, and Isobel, tired of it, walked slowly back up the beach. As she passed their encampment of rugs, Nancy, dozing in the heat, struggled to her feet. Isobel motioned her to stay still.

'I'm just going to walk a little way along the sand-dunes.'

Nancy began to protest, but Isobel shook her head. 'No further than that corner – two minutes.' She smiled. 'There might just be a breath of wind on the top.'

Nancy had already scrambled to her knees.

'You can't go alone, ma'am, and 'tis no trouble.'

'Of course I can.' Isobel laughed. 'You can watch me all the way.'

Isobel ploughed unsteadily through the soft sand, up on to firmer ground at the top of the sand-dune. She stood for a moment, looking over the Town Salts at the village, which sat like a medieval hamlet on its little hill. Then she turned instead to gaze at the sea and began to wander along the sandy ridge.

'The end of August already,' she said to herself, and it seemed

156

as though she were walking slowly over the dunes towards great iron doors a month of footsteps away from her. As though she would walk and walk throughout September with this nightmarish image looming larger before her, until finally the doors would clang shut, imprisoning her for ever.

She reached the bend in the sand-dunes, halted obediently, and looked back the way she had come. It scarcely seemed a hundred yards; one was not, she mused, even supposed to walk a hundred yards on one's own. She turned to look at the forbidden land beyond and felt suddenly as if she had walked into a corridor of icy air. Not more than ten yards away a figure sat in the grass on the slope of the dune. A loosely bundled shape, so immobile it could not be human. Isobel felt the back of her neck prickle and her eyes water. Between the shrouding folds of material and the head-covering, where the face might have been, was nothing but shadow. Isobel found she could not speak or move. She could not breathe; the muscles of her chest seemed paralysed. She was as immobile as the shape. All her wandering in search of Philip's ghost had not prepared her for this. She was not even sure that this . . . that this was . . . What if it were angry with her? She was alone in this place with it. What if it should rise up in the air and rush towards her? As she stared at it, the folds of cloth stirred and a hand slid out towards a book lying open in the grass. The head turned and a profile came clearly into view – bone and flesh and a light, gingerish moustache.

Isobel found herself running forward and stumbled into a trough of soft sand.

'Oh!' she heard herself gasp as she fell, the sound submerged in the flurry of sand and the collision of knees and arms.

'No, *no*!' His words were almost a sob. She could see nothing. Everything was slipping and sliding. A corner of the book dug into her side, and around her she felt his arms.

'No,' she crooned to the sobbing voice, swaying on her knees, entangled in her unwieldy skirts. She tried to steady herself with her hands, but Philip was holding them, kissing them with small, dry, pent-up kisses.

'No – no – no!' Each word was punctuated with another kiss. She must not kneel to him. He tried to bend lower than she, and succeeded only in dragging her down with him.

'No!' Her whispers became alarmed as she struggled to free herself and get to her feet. But he could not bear to let go of her hands. She overbalanced again and fell against him, so that their heads collided. The stubble of his chin grazed her in a glorious scar and the scent of her was all about him.

'No, no,' they moaned softly together. It was as if there were a whole language in that one word, whose very meaning of negation was removed and absolved by their use of it, the inflections and subtleties they bestowed on it.

At last Isobel struggled to her feet. 'No!' She stretched out her hand to push him back, as he, too, tried to rise. 'The maid!' she gasped.

'Ah.' He stayed there on his knees looking imploringly up at her.

There were no running footsteps, no cries from the beach, but she did not dare to turn round, to expose the nakedness of her extreme emotion. Her dress was covered in sand, her shoes weighed down by it, her hat askew. The sky seemed to reverberate with her panting breath as she struggled for air, for a foothold in reality. Was it really Philip, or was it just a materialisation of all her accumulated emotion? She stretched her hand further out, and touched his shoulder.

'Isobel,' he whispered. Quickly, she withdrew her hand and tried to readjust her hat, but her fingers were shaking so much she only made it worse. Her mouth quivered too. The muscles in her face contorted in a longing to cry.

'Come,' she whispered stiffly. 'Come after lunch to the house.' She turned anxiously to look back along the ridge of the sand-dunes, but no one was in sight. 'I must go, they . . . Don't come anywhere near the beach.'

In a flurry of sand she turned and hurried away along the path.

'Mr Sickert? Is he a painter? Ah, I confess I haven't heard of him. How interesting. Isobel, my dear, do you know of Mr Sickert?' Aunt Jude turned enquiringly to Isobel who, silent until then, started up at this chance to speak. Her hands moved jerkily in her lap and her cheeks flushed.

'Well, the name . . . ' Her voice trailed away and she seemed to sag into silence. Philip felt disconcerted: there was not the slightest reason why she should ever have heard of Walter, yet she seemed to have a desperate desire to have done so.

At this point, Isobel's daughters came into the drawing room, dressed for the beach. It seemed to Philip that Emma hung back warily, behind her sisters, but Sophie and Maria, impressed with his having been Abroad, bombarded him with eager questions. Their enthusiasm waned, however, when they learned that he had not been in Paris and that Étaples was not in the least fashionable, having almost as little society as Walberswick.

'You should have stayed here,' remarked Maria.

'I should have greatly preferred to,' replied Philip gallantly, smiling at her and then glancing past her at her mother. A glow of pleasure rose in Isobel's face, the soft smile of serenity that had captivated him from the beginning. His unease dissolved.

When the little girls had left, Philip rose to make his farewells. Aunt Jude held on to his hand as he bent to take his leave of her.

'We really haven't talked at all,' she wheezed at him. 'You must come to see us for longer. You must come to lunch tomorrow – mustn't he, Isobel.'

Isobel smiled and nodded, but her hands twisted themselves in her lap as though they did not believe he would be there tomorrow.

'You must earn your lunch, however.' Aunt Jude shook his hand as if to make him pay attention. 'You must bring us your paintings of France, Philip dear, to justify your absence from us for so long. We have been quite dull without you; now you must entertain us.'

'I'm afraid I've almost nothing to show you. I left half a dozen small oils, which was the main body of work that I completed in Étaples, plus one or two Walberswick things, with the Grosvenor Gallery on Friday, before I came down here. They're having an exhibition later this month and might choose one or two pieces of mine to show.'

'Well, well!' Aunt Jude beamed proudly at him, as though he were one of her nephews, and released his hand. 'What a famous painter we have in our midst, Isobel!'

Philip looked across and saw, with a slight shock, the some-what stupefied look of proud adoration on Isobel's face. To dim such overt expression of her feelings, Philip hastily added, 'Of course, it's not certain whether they'll take any at all.'

But Isobel seemed not to have heard him. He turned away from her to engage the attention of her aunt until she had composed herself. 'I do,' he said, 'have several water-colour sketches and some oil exercises that I would be delighted to show you, but you mustn't be too disappointed in their sketchiness. They're only plans or ideas, working in rough, for the final pictures which are now with the gallery.'

'Yes, of course,' said Aunt Jude, though he knew she had not really understood him. A picture was a picture; the idea of one being a sketch for another was irrelevant.

'Until tomorrow,' smiled Philip. He turned to Isobel. 'Until tomorrow, Mrs Heatherington.'

Isobel held on to his hand for an unnervingly long time. Outwardly, she seemed merely to place her fingers lightly on the palm of his hand so that he could bow over them, but out of sight, at the back of his hand, she was gripping him hard between the tips of her fingers and thumb.

'Goodbye,' said Philip, to prompt her into releasing him, and pulled his hand away.

As he walked back to the inn he could think only of the boldness of Isobel's farewell. It had no brightness in it, no panache to distract the watcher's gaze, only a clinging desperation that turned her fingers to iron claws. This desperation, which he could not remember noticing before, had seemed at certain moments to overcome her, slipping out of her control to twist her hands in her lap or fix her eyes in an anxious stare. It was as if she no longer cared whether they were observed – and this thought, far from exciting him, shocked Philip profoundly. It forced him to realise the dangers of the emotions they had aroused in each other. He could rely on himself, now, to keep his feelings under control, but it had not occurred to him that he would ever manage to arouse such love in a woman that she would find it difficult to keep her feelings within the bounds of propriety. The Isobel of early summer was not this Isobel. It was all his fault. He should have written – but no, he could not have written, it would have been improper. Bending his head guiltily to the road, he walked slowly past 'The Anchor' and on out of the village to the heath.

Down on the beach, Emma stood listlessly at the edge of the water while her sisters hunted in the shallows for shells and pebbles to adorn their castle. She had been so useless at helping them build the sandcastle that she had been pushed out of the way as they constructed moats and drawbridges and dug a channel to the incoming tide, with all the expertise of a summer on the beach behind them. Emma, a little apart, stared down into the water, too, but she could see nothing; her eyes were blinded as if huge flashlights were being played into her face. On-off, on-off, tiny glints of sunlight sparkled from the waves. When she closed her eyes against this bombardment, everything went hot and red as the sun beat against her closed lids and the thudding in her head got louder and louder. If she turned away from the sea and looked at the beach it was all a white glare that made her eyes hurt too. And in and out of the white sand and the red sun danced the image of Mr Steer, smiling at her and saying soundlessly, 'Hello, Emma,' over and over again, his head lunging forward every time his lips moved, as in a nightmare. And the image of Mama, sitting on one of the sofas in the drawing room, twisting her hands together in her lap and staring at Mr Steer as though no one else in the room existed. Tears welled up in Emma's eyes. Beside her, Sophie and Maria called to each other each time they found a new shell, their voices piercing Emma's head like ear-splitting yells that echoed round the beach and made her wince with pain. She felt thirsty and sick. Her cheeks burned so that she could hardly feel the tears running down them. Why, she sobbed to herself, did Sophie and Maria have to make so much noise, and why did Mr Steer have to come back? She looked at the water lapping round her ankles and scooped up a handful, but it tasted salt. She turned and started to stumble back up the beach.

Isobel sat at her dressing-table, staring at her reflection in the mirror. Around her the house was hushed and subdued. They were not changing for dinner this evening – no one felt much like eating – but Isobel had come, out of habit, to her bedroom at the usual dressing hour. Sophie and Maria were being sent to bed early as a precaution against any infection, with warm gruel and milk for supper. In the room next to theirs Emma tossed and turned, her face flushed and hot, asking constantly for water, which Aunt Jude fed her, a teaspoonful at a time.

When they had carried Emma up from the beach she had been hardly more than a crumpled heap dangling from Dolly's arms. Isobel and Aunt Jude, running in from the terrace, had both, for a second, thought her dead. A grey pallor seemed to gleam through her face, making the sun-burned skin appear like a grimy crust over her cheeks and forehead. Sweat-soaked tendrils of hair clung to her temples. Her mouth lolled half-open, and through it her breath came in harsh rattlings as though it rose from the cavernous depths of her small body, catching on huge boulders in its path.

'She's been sick, ma'am, and fainted,' explained Dolly, her arms shaking with Emma's weight. 'I run down the beach, ma'am, but I couldn't catch her afore she fell.'

'Emma, Emma!' Isobel had called in a low voice, stroking the hot face. The eyelids had fluttered, the tip of the tongue tried to lick the dry lips.

'Did Emma say she felt ill?' Aunt Jude had asked Sophie and Maria, who hung back behind Dolly, and they shook their heads.

'She was playing by herself,' disclaimed Maria, and her sister added quickly, 'I saw her drink some sea-water.'

Aunt Jude was with Emma now. Isobel began to take the pins out of her hair and watched it fall curl by curl on to her shoulders. Strange how she was taking it all so seriously; children were frequently sick. She turned to watch her hair fall down her back. If Philip could see her now . . . She smiled at the reflection of the cascade of hair, glinting in the low sunlight, and then her expression became taut and anxious. Philip. He had said nothing. Of why he went away, or why had had never written. He hadn't even tried to snatch a moment alone with her. They hadn't spoken of anything that mattered. Of what they were going to do. She thought of the fervour of his kisses on the sand-dune. She spread out her hands and looked down at them, turning them over and over. Here – and here. She held the back of one hand to her cheek as though transferring the kisses, and then, watching herself in the mirror, slowly drew her fingers across her lips. There – and there. She longed to conjure him up into the silence of the room. Why did he do nothing!

She leapt up from her chair and paced to the window, beating with her fists against the glass. He had been so passionate out on the sand-dunes and so reticent when he came to the house. He had to declare himself. She had waited and waited – she could not be silent any longer. She must see him before tomorrow. She could not endure a polite lunch with her aunt constantly in attendance without – *knowing*. She brushed her tears away impatiently. She must get a message to him. She stared out of the window for some time, as though mentally composing one, and then shook her head. It was impossible; it would arouse immediate suspicion if she sent one of the maids to 'The Anchor' with a letter. What if he were out on the heath? She scanned the common, pacing, almost running between the two windows in her room, but there was no sign of him. Suddenly, it occurred to her that he might have gone down to the pier, where they used to meet in the early evening. She seized a shawl and ran out of the room.

Although Emma had dropped into a fitful sleep, Aunt Jude continued to sit beside her, calmly pulling up the bedclothes every time Emma pushed them away. It was good, she thought, that Emma slept, albeit so restlessly. Sleep was a good sign. She settled back in her chair. But it was surprising that Isobel did not come to the bedside. She heard Emma begin to mutter, half-sounds running together inaudibly. Fever, thought Aunt Jude. The little girl fell silent. Then her hands shot out as though to push away the sheets. Aunt Jude leant forward to straighten the bed, but Emma's hands were pushing violently at empty air. Perplexed, Aunt Jude put her hands over Emma's to calm her, but she only clutched fiercely at her aunt's fingers, digging in her small nails and clenching her teeth in an attitude of hate. Aunt Jude had to struggle to disentangle her hands, and watched uneasily as Emma's fingers, deprived of their prey, dropped to the bed and scrabbled at the sheet, each appearing to quest in a different direction at once, like a nest of blind snakes.

Aunt Jude sat on at her bedside apprehensively, while the late afternoon light crossed the room into evening and shadows hung in the corners of the window. And still she could not think why Isobel did not come. Emma's flushed cheeks had turned very pale; now and then her eyelids fluttered, but the eyes remained shut. Then the muttering began again; it rose and fell and formed itself into ever clearer words. Crumpled, jumbled, tumbling out, catching on each other, falling into small silences. Aunt Jude listened, with ice at the pit of her stomach, as the incoherent story of the summer pieced itself together. At first she did not see the significance of Emma's repetition of the two names, the recurring phrases, the little, breathless fears; of going off, of being alone, of being left, of looking, of smiling, of touching hands. It was the repetition of the words that gradually sank into her brain until she found herself saying them under her breath. Philip – and Isobel? It wasn't possible. But even as she had whispered it she saw just how possible it had been. In her numbed brain a small, white-hot centre began to glow. It had been possible because she had made it so. The glow spread, fanned by a rush of memories so vivid and so damning that she gasped out loud and put one hand over eyes that prickled with tears. She sat, slumped in her chair, completely overcome by a sense of failure; her whole bulk dwindled to hide behind her hand.

The reason for her being here at all had been to act as chaperone. Instead, her frivolousness and enthusiasm had engineered the whole tragedy. She had wanted Isobel to have a friend – her husband was not a friend – and Philip had seemed safe and suitable. She had been amused by their shyness with each other, like young children at their first party, and she had pushed them together without once thinking that they might be adults of blood and flesh. She had become so taken up with her own friendship with Mr Smytheson that she had become careless. But she had never wanted this! She had not thought for a moment – Aunt Jude could not now contain her tears. She had not . . . she had never thought that they . . . And then the fire in her head turned to rage. They! They were responsible for this tragedy, not her! They had taken advantage of her generosity of nature, her belief in their innocence. Isobel, her favourite niece, who had always been so meek! And Philip – that masquerade of shyness and quietness. Ah, yes, it was not for nothing that people said to each other, look out for the quiet ones. They watch and watch and plot their subversion:

they had watched her, watched her like thieves, to steal away her good name by their foul deeds. She thought of the tainting of her reputation in her family, of her nieces whispering to one another in surprise of how Aunt Jude, of all people, had let such a tragedy . . . But no matter how vigilant she might have been they would have found a way. They were intent on it – intent on each other.

Oblivious of Emma, Aunt Jude hurled herself out of her chair, marched across the room and flung open the door. In the twilight of the passage she caught sight of Isobel on the landing, one hand against the wall, as though steadying herself, a silk shawl trailing from the other; one foot was poised above the stair in the very act of descending. Aunt Jude saw all this in a split second and, while Isobel was still balanced to begin her descent, rushed across the landing.

'Where are you going?' she thundered.

Isobel pressed herself against the wall, terrified into silence, her mouth open, her neck arched strangely back as though in an attempt to push herself through the wall. Her eyes were wild, almost half closed. She tried to draw the hand holding the shawl behind her into the folds of her dress. But her aunt seized it by the wrist and shook it in front of her face, so that the filmy material billowed out as gaudy evidence.

'Where?'

The word reverberated like a pistol shot through the silent house. Isobel pressed herself further against the wall, her mouth opening and closing, panting in her fright.

'Where?' hissed Aunt Jude. 'Where?' She began to drag Isobel across the landing.

'I must go out.' Isobel struggled to free herself from her aunt. 'I must – '

They had reached the door of Emma's room. Her fever abated, the child now lay still and sleeping. Aunt Jude pushed Isobel inside.

'You should be here!'

Isobel cast a frightened glance around the room, as though she had never seen it before, and ran out again.

'Air – I must have some air – '

Before she could reach the landing, her aunt caught her and, gripping her by one arm, pushed her past the stair-head.

'Here then!'

In front of Isobel's door they struggled once more, but Isobel was helpless against the violence of her aunt's rage. Inside the room, Aunt Jude released her and leaned heavily back against the door to close it. Her niece, recoiling, staggered backwards to one of the long windows and, pressing against it, clutched at the curtain.

'I must go out,' she whispered.

'Where?' Her aunt advanced on her. 'Where?' The words came out between clenched teeth, full of hate. 'You have a daughter who is ill, ill with a fever, yet in her fever she has seen more clearly than any of us. Under the influence of this fever she has told me *everything*! Everything about you and – ' Aunt Jude was now within six inches of Isobel. She grasped her by the shoulders and began shaking her. Isobel's head banged on the glass.

'You and – '

'What?' cried Isobel.

'Everything!' screamed Aunt Jude.

Isobel shook her head wordlessly.

'Everything!'

Isobel burst into tears, turning her head into the curtain. Her aunt dropped hold of her arms and marched back to the door.

'You are not fit,' she hissed into the weeping space, but she could not bring herself to finish the sentence and left the room, slamming the door behind her and turning the key. She stood in the shadows of the passage and heard footsteps run across the room and a faint knocking begin.

'No, no, aunt,' she heard Isobel cry.

She stood in the passage, head bowed, and thought only of her own stupidity. After some time the knocking ceased; the springs of the bed creaked suddenly as Isobel flung herself down, and through the cracks in the door came the sound of sobbing. Quietly, too quietly for Isobel to hear it above her tears, Aunt Jude turned back the key and walked slowly away.

Chapter Fifteen

Philip received the two letters together.

'Quite a postbag this mornin', sir,' said the maid as she set down his breakfast tray on the table near the window.

'Letters?' murmured Philip absently, wandering over to the table.

'Yessir, and a nice day for colourin' too, sir, if I may so,' she added, curtseying as she closed his bedroom door.

He picked up the letters and turned them over in his fingers as though they were strange objects. One was redirected to him from London. The other bore no postmark or stamp; beside his name were written the words 'MOST PRIVATE AND CONFIDENTIAL', underlined so deeply that the nib of the pen had scored into the paper. It was an old-fashioned, looping hand. Not Smytheson's hand. A handwriting that he did not know. Slowly he opened the envelope and read the note it contained. He opened the other letter. It was even shorter than the first. Then he folded both notes together and placed them carefully under the tray. The envelopes dropped unheeded to the floor. Philip sat down in front of the table. Resting his chin on his hand, he stared out of the window for a long time without registering what he saw or being aware of any thought in his head. All was just blankness. He did not hear the opening or closing of the bedroom door as twice the maid came to clear his tray and twice left empty-handed.

When at last he came to himself he was surprised at the silence around him. His world had crashed and yet there was no noise of falling. Rather, did life seem suspended, the village outside unnaturally silent as though it knew of his disgrace and had turned away from him. Tentatively, with one finger, he touched the ends of the letters that stuck out from under the tray, as though they were a wound in himself, that he deliberately wanted to make bleed. He thought of his studio in Tite Street, lined with canvases, their painted faces turned to the wall. They were ten rows deep in places. Shannon, coming into the studio one day, had whistled through his teeth, 'You're prolific!'

Philip could remember staring down at the stretchered backs and shaking his head. 'They don't sell,' he had replied. 'There's over seven years' work here.'

'But you're good!' Shannon had remonstrated, 'you're one of the best of us – you and Sickert, you're the leaders!'

It was all very well for Shannon to say that. It didn't stop his work being refused by the Academy every other year or, when it was shown, being skyed so high no one could see it. It didn't stop the private galleries rejecting him, or the critics ignoring him for months on end and then ridiculing him. It didn't stop pictures being returned unsold. He was tired of it all, sick of rejection, sick of failure; he had devoted his life to painting and life had refused to take him seriously. Instead, it sat clerks on high-stools, put pens in their hands and dictated to them unctious phrases of rejection – clerks who probably couldn't tell a Whistler from a Giorgione. He was washed up. Had this final rejection been written by one of those clerks? The signature on the letter was somehow too florid for a clerk. Had it been the gallery owner himself, watched approvingly by the second-rate old masters on his office walls?

The signature on the other letter had appeared to him for a moment to be that of an utter stranger. It was only when he read the letter itself that he realised instantly who 'Judith Catesby' was. And when he did, the hurt of it sank deeper than ever. Aunt Jude, he whispered to himself, and he saw again how unceremoniously and affectionately she had always greeted him. How she used to turn to him whenever he entered the room with always the same laugh of emotion, her eyes twinkling, her hands clapped together. It was the same laugh that his mother gave whenever he arrived in *her* house, a kind of joyous catch in the throat. It was as if his mother wrote to debar him from her house and her acquaintances. His first reaction had been the ice-cold shock of exposure. His first thought, how had she discovered it? And then, how *much* had she discovered? And then, immediately, fear for Isobel, the acuteness of which dissolved into perplexity: had she – *could* she have told her aunt?

'Mrs Heatherington and her family will be returning to

London in the next few days.' Aunt Jude controlled them all now, with an iron coldness. There was a horror about the polite iciness of her letter which crushed him utterly. He dared not show his face near Quay House again. If he were to brazen it out . . . 'We shall not be receiving,' she had written. If he were to turn up at the house to inquire after Emma's illness, which was used as an excuse for their hasty departure, he would, he knew, be turned away at the door. And by the very maids who, even yesterday, had had instructions to admit him whenever he might call. The shame, the insult – it was almost worse than the reason behind such instructions. Nothing improper had happened. It had been thought, it had been longed for, but nothing . . . The injustice of it struck him so hard it took away his breath.

He was condemned anyway; it was useless to protest. He was out somewhere in no-man's-land, in a kind of silent limbo with no point to his life and now no diversion from it either. He got up and walked round the room. He opened the doors of his wardrobe and stared at the clothes hanging there. Then he moved back to the table and ran his hand over the litter of paint-brushes and pencils. Had he failed them, or had they failed him? What was he to do with his life, now?

He wanted to see Isobel, he wanted to find out if she repudiated him as utterly as had her aunt. He thought of the yearning in her eyes the day before – it was not possible that she could change so quickly. He wanted to hear from her that she still loved him, that she did not reject him, that all this was not her doing. He stood still in front of the door, reluctant to open it, and wondered how many other people knew what had happened. He crept out on to the landing. There was no one there. He tiptoed down the stairs, ran silently along the dapple-shadowed passage and out into the village street. His relief at having escaped without notice gave way to a certainty that the staff of the inn had been avoiding him, and then that the emptiness of the village street was sinister. He was sure that he was watched from every cottage window, and that they were whispering about him. At the first opportunity, he slipped through a gap in the hedge, skirted the wide field and dropped down on to the marsh.

From here he could look straight across the Town Salts to

Quay House. The soft, rose-coloured house had opened itself to the sun all summer long. Now it was closed like a fortress among the ruins of its garden. Philip thought of Isobel shut in and himself out. What had happened in that house? Who had – ? In his anxiety he crept closer through the reeds, which waved their plumes above him as though signalling to watchers in the house: here he is, here he isss . . . But the windows of the house had a blankness to them, as if it were no longer inhabited. Philip turned and made his way towards the sea, clambering up the sand-dunes, and halting on their summit to glance over his shoulder at the village. Leaded eyes glittered back at him, hard and accusatory. Like a fugitive, he turned and ran.

All afternoon he walked along the deserted beach, down near the water where the sand was firmer and darker on the eye than the fragmented glare of bleached pebbles along the tide-line. The surface of the water seemed thin, as though it might crack and separate. It lapped, glassy-grey, near his feet, mirroring the pallor of the sky. He walked and walked but the shore seemed endless. And all the time he thought. Of Isobel and of his painting. Sometimes he would halt in his tracks for minutes together, without being aware of what he did, talking to himself, working out a particular train of thought. Or he would sit down, suddenly, on the sand and stare into the sea, probing the waves for answers, now and then burying his head on his arms in torment.

It was, he concluded, all the result of taking risks. It had all happened because he had been unwise enough to allow his emotions to express themselves. But who could not look at Isobel and feel . . . who could be with her and not . . . ? And she, if she had not loved him too, things would not have developed. There would have been nothing to develop. It was true for his painting as well. He painted what he felt. He painted – and all of him opened up. He had never painted only what they had told him to see. He painted it all: the response of every sense to whatever was before his canvas. He flung out his arms towards the sea as though embracing it for the last time, and then sank his head on his knees again. The others in his group all admired him for what he did, he knew that, at the bottom of his heart. But none of them followed him into these other dimensions of paint. They stayed where it was safe, where they had been taught to stay. Where the public wanted them to stay. Where, God knows, it was no doubt more comfortable to stay.

Philip lifted his head and saw how the sea was already subdued with the coming of evening. If he were allowed to have any sort of life when this was all over, he would never again leave the comfort of safety. But first – he stood up – there was Isobel.

He lurked on the perimeter of the village during the next two days like a pariah, wandering on the heath and over the common, watching from the marsh and waiting among the sand-dunes, but he never once caught sight of Isobel or her family. Towards evening he would judge it safe to come closer to the village and would circle the outlying cottages, sniffing, as it were, for scraps of propitious moments, sidling along the shadows of walls. It was on the second of these evenings that he thought he saw Dolly Brown ahead of him among the cottages. He thought he saw her turn and stare at him over her shoulder. He tried to shout to her, but he was out of breath and no sound came. Then she vanished into the shadows of a doorway higher up the lane, and by the time he got to where he thought he had seen her, there was no one to be found. Silence engulfed everything and he began to doubt that he had ever seen her at all.

By the evening of the third day, Philip had almost given up all hope of ever seeing Isobel again. When Mrs Pearce came to clear his supper tray she found him staring out of his window on to an already darkening landscape.

'The nights is drawin' in all of a sudden,' she remarked, clattering plates and dishes together as she loaded the tray and picked it up. The figure by the window didn't move. 'You'll be feelin' dull without your friends.'

It was the first reference anyone had made to the matter. They stared at each other across the room. Into the silence came the faint, concise sound of horses' hooves growing louder; the creaking of heavy wheels lurched past the inn and the sounds diminished again into the twilight.

'That's William with his chaise, brought Mr Heatherington from the station.' She rested the tray on the back of a chair,

171

her eyes gleaming with excitement. 'Come down to fetch them away with him tomorrow morning to London. Come down to help his missus on account of the little one being ill, I shouldn't wonder.'

Something in her stance, waiting there with the tray in front of him, seemed to demand an answer. He was vaguely aware that his answer was meant to enhance her reputation among the gossips of the village.

'Yes,' he said lamely.

She turned away towards the door. 'Mind you close your window before you light your lamp, you'll have them midgies in!'

Early next morning Philip went down to the beach to look for a place among the dunes from where he could watch Quay House. But the waiting became unbearable and, despite the clumps of marram grass behind which he attempted to hide, he felt himself ridiculously exposed to anyone who might look in his direction. Down on the marsh he felt no more protected from view, but he was unable to stay still: anxiety whispered constantly in his head. He circled ever closer to the house in a panic of perpetual movement. The morning dragged on. He was not sure what he was going to do. He began to be afraid of missing their departure, and it was only with great difficulty that he restrained himself from going to stand on the road beside the gate of Quay House. At least there he would catch a last glimpse of her, touch the hub-cap of her chaise, call out to her. For a moment all that mattered was to see her; he must see her once more. As quickly as his wildness flared up it died again, smothered by fear, and to put a safe distance between himself and the house he turned away and crossed the stream that ran through Town Flats, climbing up the hill towards the village. Below the cottages the grass grew long, dotted with thorn-bushes and clumps of thistles. Here he found a patch of sun-baked earth and sat down to wait.

From here he saw the carter manoeuvre his wagon through the gates of the house. An hour later he saw it drive away, loaded with boxes and trunks. 'They must be about to depart,' he thought, and stood up hurriedly. Then, suddenly, from the small gate of the house, a figure of a woman emerged. For a moment she hesitated by the gate; then she ran forward with small jerky steps, as though impeded by the skirts of her white travelling dress, or unsure about where it was that she wanted to go. For when she reached the other side of the road she stopped again. Then she ran on into the marsh, one hand up to her small black hat to stop it blowing away.

'Isobel!' Philip began to run down the hillside towards her. She ran on, straight ahead, in the direction of the low iron bridge that spanned the Walberswick Creek. They were running at right-angles to each other, but she seemed neither to have heard or seen him, for on the bridge she halted again, looking this way and that. And Philip stopped too, skidding to a halt in a flurry of dry earth and loose stones. Out of the driveway of Quay House sauntered a man, hands in pockets, checked deerstalker low over his forehead. He looked smaller than Philip had imagined him; nevertheless, he seemed to cover the ground between the road and the bridge extremely swiftly. On the bridge, the woman twisted this way and that, one hand clutching at a handrail, the other clutching at her hat, searching for something on the dunes or in the marsh. Philip stood motionless.

Below him, the man had already reached the bridge. As he stepped up on to it, the woman's frenzy ceased; she stood still, grasping the rail with both gloved hands, staring away from him downstream towards the estuary. It was how she had stood all those evenings on the wooden pier looking out to sea: looking for calm, she had said, in the eternity of water. The man walked past her and leaned against the railings, watching her closely. He put his hand into his waistcoat pocket and brought something out that flashed in the light. He spoke to her and she looked quickly towards the house and then back to the estuary. Philip could see the man's profile clearly. He could see the lips move and the head arch back so that the whole body was an arrogant curve beside the taut lines of his wife's shoulders and elbows. She went on staring stubbornly away from him. He lifted one foot to rest it on one of the lower rails of the bridge, his hand dangling at his waist, the thumb hooked into his waistcoat pocket. The tension between them was becoming unbearable. Trickles of sweat ran down Philip's back. It was like watching the baiting of a very small, defenceless animal, an animal cornered that finally can only turn to face its death.

And turn she did, so suddenly that Philip gasped and the man laughed. She raised tiny, knotted fists and the laugh floated out over the marsh. It all hung there for an instant, the image and the sound, and then she covered her face with her hands.

Philip sank down into the long grass and stared at the baked surface of the ground in front of him for a long time. He passed his hand over it once or twice, smoothing away the debris. Then, almost absent-mindedly, he picked up a broken twig and began to scratch on the earth's surface the figures of a man and a woman.

ANITA MASON

THE RACKET

Brazil – exploitation and corruption are the name of the game but Rosa, a conscientious teacher, tries to lead a principled, untroubled life. Until she unwittingly falls foul of a powerful businessman and his illegal plans to mine gold on an Indian reservation. And then cousin Fabio turns up, young, amoral and on the run from a very shady racket . . . Memorably recreating the dusty highways and lush jungles of Brazil, this gripping novel probes the limits of integrity in a mire of greed, poverty and plunder.

'As refreshing, well-observed and original a novel as any reader could wish for . . . moving and thought-provoking'
Daily Telegraph

'A tense and powerful picture of South America. Her spare prose manages to capture an atmosphere of breakneck inflation and universal corruption, of teeming cities and inhospitable plains'
The Independent

'The reader is swept down a white-water river of narrative . . . Like Graham Greene, whom this book in many ways evokes, Mason is good at telling stories'
The Listener

'Has the pace of a thriller and confronts the tremors of a society founded on exploitation'
The Observer

'Mason lays claim, as too few of her contemporaries are prepared to do, to the grand territory of good and evil . . . In doing so she avoids both sentimentality and the lure of overblown conclusions'
Times Literary Supplement